A girl had ~~~~ ~~~~ scratch every so often

And there were so few men able to oblige. At least not in the way Jacinda wanted—good sex with no strings attached. Wasn't that exactly what Gideon was offering? So why was she resisting?

"You don't have dinner plans, do you?" Gideon asked now, leaning close enough to kiss her neck.

With him, the sex could be simple and fun. They wouldn't talk about a *relationship*. And after his business was done, he'd be gone again. Just like Vegas... Memories of that steamy weekend could still make her sweat.

And she had a really sensitive spot just behind her ear, the one his lips were almost touching....

She turned her head, relishing the heat of his stare, the interest and honesty in his eyes. "I do if you want to take me somewhere."

Dear Reader,

Have you ever done something impulsive and crazy? Something you deeply regretted later? Or maybe even wished had never happened in the first place? My heroine, Jacinda Barrett, certainly has, and her scandalous past is now about to land squarely in her staid, respectable present.

Though I've never made a mistake as sexy and exciting as Jacinda's, I can relate—as I'm sure we all can—to being blindsided by the unexpected. Such as that time your boss walked up behind you just as you made a not-so-nice comment about his management skills. If only your boss had been a gorgeous adventurer like Gideon, I think we could all agree life would be much easier.

Feel free to e-mail me about this story or any other and check out my upcoming releases at my Web site, www.wendyetherington.com. You can contact me via regular mail at P.O. Box 3016, Irmo, SC 29063.

Happy reading!

Wendy Etherington

WENDY ETHERINGTON
What Happened in Vegas...

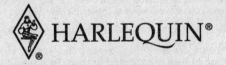

HARLEQUIN®

TORONTO • NEW YORK • LONDON
AMSTERDAM • PARIS • SYDNEY • HAMBURG
STOCKHOLM • ATHENS • TOKYO • MILAN • MADRID
PRAGUE • WARSAW • BUDAPEST • AUCKLAND

ISBN-13: 978-0-373-79389-1
ISBN-10:   0-373-79389-8

WHAT HAPPENED IN VEGAS...

www.eHarlequin.com

Printed in U.S.A.

ABOUT THE AUTHOR

Wendy Etherington lives in South Carolina with her husband and two daughters. She is the author of more than fifteen books, and though she has been lucky enough to be nominated for several prestigious awards, even winning a couple, none of them have been for exotic dancing in Las Vegas.

Books by Wendy Etherington

Don't miss any of our special offers. Write to us at the following address for information on our newest releases.

Harlequin Reader Service
U.S.: 3010 Walden Ave., P.O. Box 1325, Buffalo, NY 14269
Canadian: P.O. Box 609, Fort Erie, Ont. L2A 5X3

To my editor, Wanda Ottewell. If you weren't so damn brilliant, I wouldn't be losing you. Congrats on the promotion, girl! No one deserves it more.

1

JACINDA BARRETT dropped into the chair behind her desk with an uncharacteristic plop. "Wasn't I just here?"

Her assistant, Andrew, handed her a cup of coffee. "We all were, honey. The auction has everybody hopping." He leaned over her desk and whispered conspiratorially, "I think even the boss man stayed after five last night."

Jacinda sipped coffee to hide her smile. If Sherman Pascowitz, chairman of Callibro's Auction House since before Moses parted the seas, worked late, then the auction that was due to take place in less than a week must truly be extraordinary. And that fact added to her anxiety. She was only an assistant curator. This was the first time she'd been given the opportunity to take charge of an auction—and that was no doubt because her boss was currently on maternity leave. Still, Mr. Pascowitz could have chosen any one of the three other assistants.

"How many more items do we have to inventory?" she asked Andrew.

"About a hundred."

"Then let's hope this caffeine kicks in soon. Let me answer my e-mail, then we'll get to it."

Andrew spun and headed toward the door. "I'm there for you as always."

Jacinda didn't hide her smile this time. She faced her computer and began the process of sorting through her mail.

Andrew was an amazing asset to her office—and no doubt one of the main reasons she'd risen to the attention of the chairman after only working at the auction house for two years. Andrew was an NYU grad with an amazing eye for antiques. He was also a future fashion icon, at least as he told it.

Frankly, she thought his chartreuse suits and purple striped pants paired with sober dove-gray shirts were a bit over-the-top. But nobody—even the wildly conservative Mr. Pascowitz—seemed to care, since Andrew was completely brilliant.

Though she'd graduated at the top of her class, double majoring in history and business, she'd done so at University of Nevada, Las Vegas, which wasn't exactly Harvard. And her family's history involved lots of cocktail waitresses. Andrew came from big money, so he grew up with class, plus he was one of those IQ-off-the-scale people. She'd lucked out in a big way by having him assigned to her.

She was nearly through her inbox when the intercom beeped.

"Ms. Barrett, do you have a moment to meet with a potential client?" Andrew asked.

Andrew only addressed her formally when he had a VIP in the office, so Jacinda had to fight back a groan. She barely had half a cup of coffee in her. "Of course. Send him in."

Seconds later, the door to her office opened and Andrew strode in, followed by another man. A *gorgeous* man wearing faded jeans and a white T-shirt. A man who had shoulder-brushing, black wavy hair, green eyes and a sculpted jaw.

A man she recognized.

Damn, damn, damn.

Half out of her chair, Jacinda swallowed her fears and held out her hand, praying she'd changed enough, hoping like crazy that enough time had passed and that a certain weekend in Vegas had been easily forgotten.

No such luck.

Their hands connected along with their gazes. Recognition sprang into his, followed by sexual awareness and amusement. "Ms. Barrett," he said smoothly.

"Ms. Barrett, this is Gid—"

"Oh, she knows who I am," Gideon Nash said, still staring into her eyes, still holding her hand.

Resisting the instinct to melt into a puddle as she desperately shoved aside memories of hot skin, heavy breathing and intense satisfaction, Jacinda pulled her hand back. She glanced at Andrew long enough to see his eyebrows lift, then he winked and left the room.

Jacinda, who'd run from a fight exactly *once* in her life, nearly ran after her assistant.

"Does he always dress like that?" Gideon asked, glancing back as the door clicked shut.

"Yes."

"Is he color-blind?"

"Not that I'm aware of."

"Okay. Takes all kinds, I guess." He faced her again. His gaze slid from her face down her body, leaving burn marks in its wake.

She fought against his allure, against memories she

had no business recalling. It was as if the past six years faded away in a single moment. But, beneath the desire that somehow, inexplicably, hadn't diminished, was an odd combination of fear and anger.

Hadn't she fought, clawed and finessed her way out of her old life? Hadn't she convinced herself wild, impulsive decisions led nowhere productive? Didn't she now have the respectability she'd always longed for? Weren't all the sacrifices worth her own office, an assistant and her first auction?

He settled into the chair in front of her desk. "I always thought that 'it's a small world' expression was a bit trite, but here we are living it."

She remained standing. Every advantage seemed vital at the moment. "I guess we are."

His gaze flicked over her again. "You're different."

"You're not."

She remembered the same half smile on his face as he'd gazed up at her on the Vegas club stage where she'd danced for college tuition money, where she'd been anonymous and bold. Exotic and sensual. Half-dressed. Cheap. Hiding her ambition behind a stage name and thick layer of hair spray and lip gloss.

"What happened to Jacy Powers?" he asked, his voice deep and husky, just as she remembered it.

"Gone. She's not coming back."

"What a shame. I liked her."

She closed her eyes briefly. *Dear heaven.* "I didn't." Opening her eyes, she forced herself to glare at him. "What do you want?"

"Is that any way to talk to a potential benefactor?"

Digging deep for the elegance she'd fought so hard to

cultivate, she eased herself into her chair. "No, but since you're not one, I feel perfectly comfortable being direct."

"Oh, right. I forgot." He smiled. "I'm just an adventurer chasing a pipe dream."

Yet she'd still been tempted to follow him. She'd actually considered trading her future and her dreams for this man. "Aren't you?"

"Most of the time. Aren't you going to ask if I ever found the Diamond of Sierra?"

She fought the urge to roll her eyes. *Talk about a pipe dream.* "Did you?"

"Yes."

Despite herself, she was impressed. During the brief time they'd spent together, he'd assured her he was well on his way to finding great treasure and achieving fame. Though their chemistry was fantastic, and he was charming and fun, she hadn't believed a word he said. He'd shared too many characteristics with the endless parade of guys through Vegas's casinos with dollar signs in their eyes and surefire plans to beat the house.

Now, however, she recognized how different he'd been from those dreamers. His plans had relied not on the luck of the draw but on solid research. She also recognized that a gem of the size and fame of the Sierra could bring a great deal of publicity to her auction. "Do you still have it?"

"You'd probably like to have it in your upcoming auction."

She leaned back in her chair. This was why he'd come. He wasn't trying to dig up the past and jeopardize her reputation. He was looking to make money. She'd be glad to accommodate him. "Naturally."

"Sorry. I sold it soon after I acquired it." He angled his head. "I'm surprised you didn't take notice."

After their wild weekend together, she'd thought about double-checking his claims. She'd nearly approached the friend who'd introduced them about a hundred times to ask her the whole story about the sexy, mysterious Gideon Nash.

But Jacinda had only been into that weekend for fun. She wasn't like her mother, who actually *believed* the stories and promises men told her. Plus, Jacinda hadn't wanted it getting around the club that she'd become sexually intimate with a customer. She'd needed that job, and Gideon was way too big a risk. Years later her discretion had paid off, since her boss agreed to tell people she'd been a waitress when potential employers—especially high-dollar ones like the auction house—called her references.

"I thought it was best to make a clean break," she said.

"I expected you at the airport."

Jacinda shook her head. "No, you didn't." Laying her hands on her desk, she forced herself to calmly link her fingers. "Why don't you tell me why you're here?"

"I want to see the emerald."

"What em—" She clenched her hands as she realized the auction piece he had to be referring to. "The Veros family emerald?"

He smiled, but the expression didn't reach his eyes. "Yes, that one."

Though curious about his interest in the stone, she knew there was no way he had the kind of money necessary to actually *buy* the emerald. Who turned treasure hunter/aimless adventurer into a profitable profession?

She managed a polite smile. "The auction is next week. If you'd like a catalog—"

He stood. "I want to see the emerald now."

"We don't do previews. The auction—"

"Yes, you do. For VIP clients." He paused, his gaze hitting hers like a laser. "I'd think you'd be glad to do a favor for an old friend."

"You're not a friend."

"No, I was much more." He angled his head. "Or was I?"

Visions of slick skin, rippling muscles and blazing green eyes raced through her mind. Over the years there were moments she was sure she could smell him, moments she just *knew* he'd been in her car, or her apartment. He never was, of course. But the memories of them together were so strong, so vivid, she couldn't completely set them aside. No matter how hard she fought.

"We weren't anything," she said.

He clutched his hands over his heart. "Aw, now my feelings are hurt."

"I don't want to get into a confrontation with you."

"Then don't. Show me the emerald."

She sighed in the face of his determination. Maybe he'd heard the rumors about the gem's beauty, wanted to see it and had hoped to charm the auction director into allowing the viewing. Now he was using their linked past to push his way into the vault. Maybe the stone had been lost once-upon-a-time, and he'd tried to find it. Maybe a competitor had beaten him to its recovery.

Hell, maybe he'd tried to steal, swindle or connive the emerald from somebody and failed.

She *should* toss him out of her office. She *should* plant

her foot and call security to get him out. In six years, she *should* have found the strength to say no to him. Instead, she was tempted to grant his request.

Why?

For old time's sake? A thanks-for-the-two-hot-nights parting gift?

As much as she'd like to assign a complicated reason or a justification for breaking the rules, she knew the real motivation was much more simple.

He intrigued her.

The way no one else ever had, from the first moment she'd laid eyes on him. He drew her toward him like the proverbial moth to a flame, tempting her toward the heat, even though the danger of burning up loomed if she made the mistake of getting too close.

Why was he here—really? Though he'd seemed surprised to see her, had he *expected* to find her when he walked into the office? If so, how had he found her? Hell, how did he *remember* her, a girl who had to have been one in a million?

And what was his connection to the valuable emerald? What did he want it for? Did he have a client on the hook, or did he merely want to gaze upon its magnificence?

She rose, making sure she did so with grace and confidence. He had to notice the differences between Jacinda and Jacy. She hoped he kept the contrast clear in his mind. She'd made a new life, and she wouldn't let him show up and jeopardize a moment of it.

What did it matter if she let him have his way and see the stone? He'd be out the door and out of her life quicker if she gave in to his request.

She rounded the desk, then headed toward the door.

Glancing over her shoulder, she smiled. "You're coming, aren't you?" she asked, since he hadn't moved.

His gaze slid from her face, down her body, then rose slowly, leisurely, again. "You always had a distracting strut."

She bit back a gasp of annoyance. Leave it to Gideon, the wild, live-for-the-moment adventurer, to steal her control and land her smack-dab in the middle of her past so effortlessly. "I don't strut." *Not anymore.*

He reached around her and opened the door. "You most certainly do."

The enticing scent of him washed over her, and the memories quickly followed, as if six minutes had passed instead of six years. She recalled the heat of his body, the way his lean muscles rippled beneath her touch, the intense pleasure he'd brought her—like none other she'd had before or since. She remembered gawking at the luxury hotel suite, the expensive dinner and champagne. All free, he'd said. A gift from a gambler friend who'd decided to head to Monte Carlo instead of Vegas that weekend.

The charming, exotic mystery of Gideon had seduced her with nothing more than a smile and the promise of a good time.

A risk that had paid off in a big way.

At least for two days.

Beyond that, she knew his offer to come away with him was empty. She danced in skimpy costumes for horny vacationers. She knew her place in the world. No matter what his grand ambitions had been, she'd had ambitions of her own. And they hadn't included skipping around the world on a friend's generosity or chasing after the next treasure.

She didn't even consider the idea that they'd be together for longer than it took boredom to set in.

And, yet, here he was.

His appearance was unexpected and curious. Something she couldn't set aside so easily. Because she'd begun to wonder if ambition really was a lonely and empty path? Because she'd had years to realize how special their brief moments together were? Or because the connection was just that strong?

"I only have a few minutes," she said finally.

"That's what you said when we got in the cab six years ago." He leaned close. "Is tonight going to turn out the same way?"

With an ease she knew she hadn't possessed the last time she'd seen him, she turned away. "Don't hold your breath."

As they walked through the outer office, Andrew was typing on his computer. "I'm going to the warehouse. I'll be back in a few minutes."

"Yes, Ms. Barrett."

God bless the man for knowing how to turn on the disinterested professionalism when necessary. More often than not, when something interesting was going on in the office, he plopped his backside on her desk and demanded that she "dish" about the news.

No doubt the dishing would come later.

After passing through several security checkpoints, both mechanical and human, Jacinda and Gideon reached the warehouse. With the upcoming auction, there were dozens of people around, checking inventory, organizing the receiving area and opening crates.

Rumor around the office said that Malle Callibro

herself—after whom the auction house was named—used to walk through the warehouse every night before she left to be sure the treasures entrusted to her were safe and sound.

"Ms. Callibro built quite an empire," Gideon commented as he looked around.

"How do you know—"

"Her name's on the marquee out front."

"Of course."

And *of course* Gideon Nash didn't know anything personal about somebody as high society as Malle, who'd broken rules, doing the unexpected and making her own way in the world. Jacinda figured rising from a cheap go-go club in Vegas to a prestigious auction house in Manhattan could be considered rule-breaking, too.

"She supposedly had over fifty lovers during her lifetime," Gideon said.

"*Supposedly* is right. With those kinds of numbers, she'd never have had time to build her business." She paused at the vault door guarding the auction house's jewelry. "Which she most certainly did."

"Personally, I prefer quality over quantity."

"No kidding." She smiled wanly over her shoulder at him. "I never would have guessed."

He moved in close behind her. "You don't consider our time together quality?"

She fought against the intimate tone of his voice, the warm, masculine scent teasing her nose. "It was…fine."

She didn't see, but could feel his smile. "*Fine*, huh?"

There was no way the words *fabulous, amazing* or *exhilarating* were coming out of her mouth. "It was just a weekend."

"Like so many before and since?"

How had he boxed her so neatly into a corner? If she said yes, she'd look like a slut. If she said no, he'd probably display some self-satisfied smirk, as if he was the greatest lover on the planet.

As far as you know, he is.

That was beside the point.

She turned her head to meet his gaze. "We've both moved on," she said neutrally. "Do you want to see the emerald?"

He drew his finger gently, slowly along her jawline. "Very much."

"Step back."

"Why?"

"I have to enter the code for the door."

He stepped away and turned his back.

She entered the code, waited a moment to be sure all the laser sensors and alarms had disengaged, then pulled open the door. The moments without his stare blazing into her also allowed her time to roll her shoulders and regain her poise. She was no longer curious about why he wanted to see the jewel. She just wanted him gone.

He reminded her of a past she'd fought like crazy to forget. He tempted her. He made her think about twisted sheets and tangled limbs—a distraction she couldn't afford.

She'd show him the gem, then hustle him out. He'd go back to chasing his pipe dreams, and she'd get back to double-checking inventory. His chaos and her order. The only way both of them would be happy.

After flipping on the lights, she walked into the small room. The walls were draped in black, lint-free fabric and the overhead spotlights simulated natural light, which showed flaws in lesser stones, but illuminated the brilliance of the superior ones. The glass display cabinets formed a *U*, inviting the viewer into the middle to goggle and sigh.

Gideon was right. She *did* bring VIP clients back here. She'd escorted five in the past week, two of whom specifically wanted to view the Veros emerald.

And though Gideon wasn't a VIP—and she was wildly uncomfortable with him smack in the middle of her respectable new life—he would appreciate the stone as much as she did. He was one of the few people who'd actually care where it came from and what it represented.

"It's in the corner," she said—unnecessarily it seemed, since Gideon was already heading in that direction.

He said nothing for several moments, and Jacinda stayed behind him, anticipating he'd like to absorb the magnificent cut and clarity on his own. Even if he really had the money to bid for it, she knew she didn't need to come up with a sales pitch. The gem's deep greenish blue color and minimal flaws detectable by the naked eye were rare and set it apart from other emeralds in an obvious way, just as the infamous Hope diamond shined not clear like common diamonds, but with blue brilliance for the millions of tourists shuffling through the Smithsonian.

The only drawback had been the Veros gem's setting. The staid gold-and-silver broach surrounding it crowded the light too much and didn't highlight the emerald. After much wrangling and begging, she'd finally convinced the family that if they wanted top bids, they'd have to allow the auction house to remove the gem from the setting, so that the buyer could see the emerald from all sides and angles.

Now the stone lay unadorned on a minimal set of prongs, raised above a cushion of black cloth.

"It's amazing," he said, barely above a whisper.

"Yes, it is."

"I've seen pictures, but I never imagined…"

She smiled, understanding his awe. It reminded her that he loved beautiful things. Beautiful, *expensive* things. And though she'd had a decent face and a lush body when they'd first met, she'd been cheap. In appearance and profession. She'd changed all that. She used her brain instead of her body now—though she still had the lush body for someone who took the time to look beneath her conservative suits—but she still felt the tarnish of cheapness. Maybe she always would.

Shoving aside her insecurities, she said, "I have a loupe and tweezers if you'd like a closer look."

"Thanks. I would."

Rounding the counter, she retrieved the necessary tools, then entered another code, allowing her access to the cabinet containing the emerald. The auction house didn't take chances with its inventory, and the emerald was one of its most valued.

She retrieved the tray containing the stone, then stepped back a bit, wanting to watch him work.

He used the tweezers and loupe like a pro, his hands looking strong and capable as the emerald shot sparks in a million directions, the stone seeming to glow from the inside like something from a mythological tale.

Oddly enough, she recalled their second night together. After they'd had amazing sex in the shower, they'd sat on the bed wearing bathrobes and eating lobster from room service. Gideon had suddenly jumped up, returning a few moments later with a black cloth, which he'd handed to her.

Inside the folded cloth was a ring, a four-karat, square-cut sapphire with diamonds surrounding it. An exquisite stone, its color deep and mysterious, like the Pacific Ocean, somehow cold and warm at the same time.

The ring had been lost, Gideon had explained, when a man had hocked it in anger after his wife divorced him. The couple had reunited recently, and the man wanted it back. He'd hired Gideon to find the ring, which he had.

But for the first time in his career, Gideon said he'd been tempted to keep a treasure. He'd slid the ring on her finger.

It's the color of your eyes....

"I want it."

The sapphire? But you gave it to your client. How—

She blinked away the past and tried to ground herself again in the present. *The emerald.* He was talking about the emerald. He wasn't here to see her. He wasn't here to give her gifts, or tease her with things she'd never have.

"I imagine you do," she said coolly as she returned the emerald and its tray to the case and locked it. "Along with dozens of other people. Feel free to bid at the auction on Wednesday."

"You don't understand. It's already mine."

"Yours?" She raised her eyebrows in disbelief. "Be serious. Is this some Adventure-Man ploy? The emerald clearly belongs—" She stopped as he handed her a stack of photographs he'd drawn from his back pocket.

For the first time, she felt a tremor of unease—*professional* unease. The man may have her sweating the personal stuff, but she was confident in her job. Nothing shook her in that area.

Yet, while she'd been dreamily reliving the past, he was all business.

Rolling her shoulders, she shuffled through the pictures. They were in black and white. The first was a doozy, showing a young, beautiful woman wearing an obviously couture gown, long white gloves and a magnificent choker around her neck being presented to the King of England.

Okay, that was...unexpected.

Where had Gideon gotten these pictures? The library? The Internet?

The photos are yellowed and rough at the edges, not recently printed.

She shook away the disturbing thought, as well as the even more unsettling vision of them being pulled from a family album, or from a box in the back of somebody's closet.

Fighting to keep her hands still, she shuffled through several more, which showed the same woman smiling and posing, dancing and bowing. The constant in all the pictures was the lovely gown and the amazing choker around her neck. The choker that featured a large, emerald-cut gem. Twenty-one karats, if Jacinda had any kind of decent eye.

And she did.

Still, the pictures were old black-and-whites. The stone in the choker could be glass. It could be any color. The pictures could be doctored. In the age of digital technology, anything was possible.

On the other hand...Jacinda was pretty sure she recognized the woman in the photos. Sophia Graystone. A high-society woman who'd been wild in her youth but who had eventually married and become one of the most respected philanthropists in the city. A close friend of Malle Callibro. In the director's office, there was even a picture of them smoking cigars in a club, laughing as if the world existed to simply amuse them.

"It's Sophia Graystone," she said to Gideon, forcing disinterest into her voice. "So?"

"The emerald in the pictures is the same you see in the display case," Gideon said.

"Oh, please. They're black-and-white photos and—"

"It's the same," he insisted.

She said nothing.

His gaze burned into hers. "Sophia was a close friend of Malle Callibro."

"So I've heard. Look, I—"

"She's also my grandmother."

2

GIDEON WATCHED Jacinda's face pale. Her hands trembled around the pictures she held.

He wanted to comfort and assure her, but there was too much at stake. Hadn't he come here for shock value? Hadn't he counted on catching her off guard?

Still, it hurt to watch her hurt.

"Sophia Graystone is my grandmother," he repeated, concerned that Jacinda needed a jolt.

Jacinda's gaze jumped to his, back to the pictures, then latched on to his again. "So, you're…you're—"

"Incredibly wealthy and privileged." He smiled gently. "Yes, I'm afraid so."

She laid the pictures on the display case and stepped back. "You lied to me."

"No, I don't think I did." He'd been careful, as always, and given her limited details. To some, his words would have been considered lying; to others, simply self-protection. "I told you I chased treasures for a living. You assumed I was a penniless and unsettled dreamer, and I—" He stopped, knowing even if he hadn't directly lied before, he needed to come clean now. "And I encouraged you to accept that assumption. I feel like I've spent half my life dodging women with their eyes on my trust fund."

She glared at him, her blue eyes as sharp as a laser. "Oh, gee, how horrible for you."

He reached for her hands; she shook her head. "Not my best explanation. I *am* an unsettled dreamer. I'm just not exactly penniless."

"Not exactly."

The word *billions* in conjunction with his family's wealth was arrogant and ridiculous, even though it was true. He'd purposely kept that truth from the Vegas dancer he'd known so intimately. After only a few hours with her, though, he'd also known she didn't need protection, that she was a remarkable, amazing woman.

Still, he'd kept silent. He'd always wondered what it would be like to be loved and accepted for *what* he was and not *who* he was. With the perfect opportunity dangling in front of him, he'd grabbed it. He'd let her assume his only ambitions were for fame and fortune.

In short, he'd lied in a big way.

Now, he admitted no small amount of shame over that decision. He'd wanted her body, had been intrigued by her mind, but he wouldn't have presented her in the drawing room of his grandmother's Park Avenue home. Was he, after all, a hypocrite?

"I'm sorry I lied to you before, though I didn't hide everything. I *do* chase down lost treasures for clients. I *am* fascinated by history and family heirlooms. I just happen to be able to bankroll my searches if I so choose. It's my way of giving back. My family encourages community service." He held up his hand. "No, that's not enough. We're *required* to give back. It's practically a family motto."

"How generous of you."

He ignored her sarcasm. He deserved it. But there was so much more at stake than mottos and past liaisons. "It's what I do."

Her eyes sparking with fiery temper, she paced away from him. "You find treasure."

"Yes."

"But not for money."

"Not usually. I do it to find lost legacies."

She stopped. "Oh, please."

"Oh, yes."

"You're just a generous and selfless kind of guy."

"Naturally."

Crossing her arms over her chest, she shook her head. "So why now? Why *this* treasure?"

He hadn't expected her to listen to him and was actually relieved she hadn't thrown him out of the building. *That* would have put a serious damper on his mission.

He needed Jacinda on his side. He needed her to believe him. Proving his claims that the emerald belonged to his family wasn't going to be easy, and it was vital to have an ally in the opposing camp. "Obviously because of the family connection. It's been a quest of mine for many years. When I saw the preview pictures of your auction, I knew I'd found it at last." He paused, figuring he might as well spill the rest of it. "Imagine how surprised I was to find your name on the contact list."

"My——" She stopped, narrowing her eyes. "You knew me as Jacy Powers."

"I knew who you really were within twenty-four hours of leaving Vegas."

Obviously embarrassed, she turned away.

"I was curious." He lowered and gentled his tone. "I'm sorry. I didn't mean to intrude."

"It doesn't matter," she said tightly, though clearly it did. She spun back to face him, her face a blank mask. "If the emerald belongs to your family, how do you think it could have possibly found its way here?"

"It was stolen from my grandmother many years ago."

"No kidding. Tragic."

Her doubtful tone set him on edge. "It was."

While he hadn't expected to be welcomed with open arms, knowing his deception about his family and the money would be revealed, neither had he expected her to be so hard and cold. He remembered the laughter and teasing challenge in her eyes. What had happened to her that changed her so much?

"You have proof of this theft?" she demanded.

"I have the original insurance claim."

"Dated nineteen-forty…"

"Nine."

"And the insurance agent can testify to that?"

"He's dead."

"I'm so sorry."

"We weren't close."

"Still, it must have been a tragic loss for your family and your…" She paused and smirked. "Legacy."

She was mistaken if she thought insulting him would get rid of him. "Are you doubting my word that the emerald was stolen from my family?"

She pursed her lips. "Mmm. Let me think…." Her gaze sliced to his. *"Yes."*

He clenched his jaw.

Passion always brought passion—in either devotion or

conflict. He could work with that. He'd made it work for him many times before. He'd hoped their past would bond them, if only a little. He'd hoped to flirt and tease his way into her good graces.

But he could be hard. Tough. Unrelenting.

His pulse hammering in his veins, he rounded the display cases and advanced toward her. He felt the weight of each step.

The closer he got, the wider her eyes became.

He'd always been charming with her. He'd been careful to be easygoing. That persona suited him.

But everything was different today.

Today, she had what he wanted. Today, she glared at him. Today, she doubted his word. Today, six years had passed since he'd touched her, since he'd felt the tension and need between them.

Today, despite all logic, distance and opposing views, he still wanted her.

As he drew closer, her body heat melded with his. The sensual perfume that was part her and part chemical reaction between them teased him. Invited him. The intimacies they'd shared flowed through him. Memories of her hot, silky skin wouldn't let go, as if she'd physically grabbed him around his throat.

Well, actually, she'd grabbed him a bit lower.

And she had *amazing* hands.

"That emerald is mine," he managed to say, his voice hoarse with suppressed desire.

"I don't think so, Adventure Boy. It's in *my* display case. It's on *my* auction roster."

"I'm not a boy."

She cocked her head. "Leave it to a guy to dispute, not

the facts, but the cheap attack on his manhood." Drawing her finger down his chest, she smiled smugly. "You've softened over the years, Gideon. What a shame."

As he grabbed her finger, he could actually feel his blood boiling. He'd tracked his family's gem for more than a decade. He'd run down false leads. He'd bribed people. He'd failed and started again. He'd been subjected to ridicule and continually fought through the doubts of his family, friends and colleagues.

With the emerald finally within his reach, with his family's honor at stake, he wasn't compromising.

Even for the sensual abandon of the woman before him.

He squeezed her finger. "As I recall you liked me hard, so any softness must be a great disappointment."

Her eyes darkened to smoke. Her lips parted.

So maybe the icy shell she'd built around her wasn't so thick after all. Maybe she did remember the heat they'd shared. How long before he could loosen the buttons of her suit, before he could reveal that lush body she was trying so hard to hide?

He'd promised himself he'd be professional, that this was not the time for sex. He'd hoped that goal would last more than twenty minutes.

She smiled, but not with invitation. "If I had any intention of picking up where we left off six years ago, I *might* be disappointed."

"I didn't offer you anything." *Yet, anyway.*

She smiled again, her eyes mocking. "Sure you did."

"So we're keeping things strictly professional?"

"This *thing* isn't going to last more than ten minutes, so, yes, I'd say so."

"You give me the emerald. I walk out of here. Okay, ten minutes sounds about right."

"Not so fast." She angled her head, looking amused. "You really think it's yours."

"I *know* it is."

She tapped one finger on his chest, then scooted around him. "Prove it."

He clenched his fists at his sides to keep from reaching for her. Or strangling her. Her amusement at his expense was infuriating. Why wasn't she wound as tight as he was? Why did one touch, one sensual smile, have him hard and aching? The moment when she'd softened—an expression reminiscent of that weekend—had been way too short.

He wanted that connection back. He wanted her horizontal for hours on end.

But not more than you want the emerald, you idiot. Charming. Think charming. Get what you want, then *worry about the rest.*

"Let's talk about it over dinner."

"I have plans for dinner."

"Then drinks." He glanced at his watch. "At six. At Thai Bistro. It's down the street."

She frowned.

"You *do* still like Thai food?"

"What difference does it make? We're just having drinks."

"An excellent point." He forced a smile. "So, we're on?"

She extended her hand, clearly indicating she wanted him to leave the vault. "Sure. Can't wait."

Like spending time with him was torture. To keep his

temper in check, he thought of his family's legacy so closely within his grasp. It had actually been in his grasp a few minutes ago. That gem held answers to his past. He wasn't letting it go. "Think of the professional contacts you could make with my family and their friends. Don't you want to spend time with Sophia Graystone's grandson?"

She pulled the door to the vault closed. The alarm reset automatically, emitting a series of beeps. "Not particularly, no."

He'd have to see what he could do about changing her mind.

JACINDA SMOOTHED her hand down her hair as she approached the entrance of Thai Bistro. Her heart was pounding ridiculously, and she couldn't get the image of Gideon's inviting smile out of her mind. Nor the memory of his hot body, and the amazing things he could do with it.

He'd tempted her beyond her boundaries before. He'd made her forget her goals of earning money for school, of working her way up to a respectable profession and life. He'd dangled the possibility of a life without rules, without structure or—at least she thought at the time— security.

To learn he had all the security—aka *dollars*—he needed, and then some, was maddening. Infuriating. And, damn it, smart. The fact that he'd lied to an exotic dancer he'd picked up for a two-night stand in Vegas was certainly understandable.

The big questions for her were more profound. Would she have given up her big plans if she'd known about his bank account during those few crazy days? Would she have followed him into the sunset and happily been his arm candy?

Would she have compromised her goals for money?

The fact that she honestly didn't know made her as edgy and irritable now as it had earlier that morning when Gideon had disclosed his family's history.

Of course, she'd thoroughly checked out him and his story. After reluctantly confessing her personal history and present regarding Gideon—leaving out the claims about the emerald, since they were too bizarre to consider—she and Andrew had scoured the Internet, hoping beyond reason to find a hole in Gideon's story, to find doubt that he was the grandson of the infamous Sophia Graystone.

Andrew, with all his high-society connections, had called a friend, who'd called a friend to get the scoop. His people had gleefully confirmed that the rebellious, not-quite-respectable, Indiana Jones–like Gideon Nash was a member of the Graystone dynasty.

Ugh.

Worse, later, when she was alone again she'd found published photos of Sophia wearing the gem that resembled the emerald currently sitting in the Callibro's Auction House vault. Scheduled to be sold in six days. For millions of dollars.

The Veros family—on record as the current owners of the emerald—and her boss, Mr. Pascowitz, were going to be seriously pissed if Gideon could prove his claims.

Then there was the personal risk to herself and her reputation. She didn't want her past—of which Gideon was an undeniable part—anywhere near her present. Last year, pictures of her boss's secretary posing in a beach bikini contest had circulated around the office with much snickering from the men and derisive comments from the women. Shortly thereafter the secretary had been fired for cause—job performance and attendance issues being cited. But in Jacinda's mind, the photos had precipitated the action.

Just imagine what response pictures of herself in glitter, barely there spandex and fishnets would instigate. The thought made her break out in hives.

The whole business was a damn mess, and yet all Jacinda could think of were hot, wild, inappropriate thoughts about the man causing all the trouble.

The man would be her downfall. She was absolutely certain of it.

As she flung open the door to the restaurant, she reflected on their earlier conversation. She *did* have plans for dinner.

One of those new spa meals from Lean Cuisine.

But she also had fantasies about spending time with Gideon. And none of them included dinner.

Dessert, maybe.

When her cell phone rang, and she recognized the number as Andrew's, she answered the call.

"Are you there yet?" he asked.

"Walking in the door."

"Do you still want me to call in an hour about your urgent appointment?"

"Definitely."

"You're weak."

"And then some."

"Honey, I would be, too, if that man looked at me the way he looks at you."

Jacinda sighed. "You're not helping."

"Oh, right. Stay strong. Keep your blouse buttoned."

"Got it."

"And definitely keep your pants buttoned."

"I'm wearing a skirt."

"Well, then—"

"Oh, man, there he is."

Andrew expelled a lustful sigh. "How does he look?"

"Same as earlier. Jeans. White T-shirt."

"Lip-smacking, in other words."

Jacinda's nipples throbbed. "Yep. Pretty much."

"Go get 'im."

She halted on her way to the bar. "Andrew!"

"Right. Don't get him—at least not physically." He paused. "Can you get him physically, tell me all the details and still have us maintain the integrity of the auction?"

"Oh, hell. I don't see how."

"Still, I'd go for it."

"You're supposed to be *helping*."

"He *is* really sexy."

"I'm hanging up now."

"As long as you call me in the morning!"

More frustrated and nervous than ever, especially knowing Andrew had no intention of calling her later to save her, Jacinda ended the call. Heading toward Gideon, she straightened her shoulders and convinced herself she could be calm and cool in his presence.

The bead of sweat rolling between her breasts belied her forced confidence, but she ignored that, too.

She could keep her job and her respectability while sharing a drink with a sexy guy. Even if that sexy guy could threaten her job and respectability. Even if he decided to play this game dirty and threaten to expose her past unless she helped him get the gem it was her responsibility to protect. Even if that guy added the temptation of another hot night or two, where rules and respectability were stifled by lingering kisses and arousing touches.

Sure, no problem.

3

JACINDA STROLLED toward Gideon as if she didn't have a care in the world and slid onto the bar stool he pulled out next to him. "Johnnie Walker on the rocks," she said to the bartender.

The guy's gaze tracked down her body, presumably taking in her pale blue Chanel suit and expensive leather bag. "That's not a very prissy drink."

"I'm not a prissy woman."

"It's nice to see a high-powered job and fancy office haven't completely tamed you," Gideon said as he returned to his seat.

She smiled slightly and accepted her drink. "No, I guess not."

"My grandmother would call you a great dame."

"Would she?" After the research she and Andrew had done all afternoon, she supposed that would be a compliment.

"She'd like you even better if you gave her back her emerald."

"It's not mine to give."

"I'll prove it belongs to my family."

"I look forward to it. Let's table that. Tell me what you've been doing the last six years."

Surprisingly, he agreed to her cop-out, for which she was grateful.

The auction had taken its toll on her stamina, and she needed a distraction from imagining the scandal if Gideon decided to go to the press with his story. Somehow, Mr. Pascowitz would manage to blame any problems on her. She'd seen him throw more than one staff member under the bus when his own back was against the wall.

Setting aside thoughts about her boss, she focused on Gideon. However strange and unsettled his life as a finder of lost legacies seemed to her, he clearly relished every minute. He'd been to exotic places she'd rarely seen pictures of, much less dreamed of exploring. While he poked through antique stores, auction houses, pawn shops and estate sales, he also spent many hours in libraries and at universities doing research.

He'd acquired an impressive art collection and learned to speak four languages. He'd interviewed everyone from royalty to the homeless. He'd located people and things that didn't want to be found. He'd made sure thieves and swindlers were prosecuted. He returned necklaces, rings and even crowns to elderly, teary-eyed ladies.

"Did they all have blue hair?"

He put on a look of mock insult. "Are you doubting the credibility of my stories?"

"You can certainly spin an excellent tale." And they were probably true, if exaggerated. "What does your upper-crust grandmother think of her treasure-hunting grandson?"

"She mostly approves." He grinned. "Though she'd rather I donated more of my finds instead of turning them over to their privileged owners. She especially didn't like me getting Marcus Capwell's watch back for him."

"You mean former Senator Capwell?"

Gideon curled his lip. "That's him."

"Why didn't she want you to get his watch back?"

"He stiffed her for the tab one night after inviting her and her friends to drinks at a club."

She angled her head in confusion. "She's ticked at him over a bar tab?"

"It was a ten-thousand-dollar tab."

"Ah. That would do it. So why did you look for it in the first place?"

"Because I'd hoped the trail would lead to some embarrassing places."

"And did it?"

He grinned. "Definitely."

"That's pretty bloodthirsty."

He toasted her with his beer bottle. "A good thing to remember when dealing with me."

She met his gaze directly. "You don't scare me, Gideon. Nothing does. Not anymore."

He laid his hand over hers, his thumb covering the pounding pulse point at her wrist. "I never thought you were anything less than absolutely brave. In fact..." He stroked her cheek. "I think you're pretty amazing."

She leaned back from his touch and looked away. "Deep down, I'm exactly the same as I was six years ago."

"A dancer?"

"A survivor."

"That's a good thing."

"Sure it is."

He inched forward, holding her jaw against his palm. "So, why are you embarrassed?"

"I'm not." She forced a smile, even as her mind walked

again through the mansions she'd visited over the past few years, each containing priceless treasures, each perfect in every decorating detail, each refined and tasteful.

Then she recalled the dingy duplex where she'd grown up: the stove that rarely worked, the stained carpet, the sputtering candles she'd light because the power was cut off every few months. The desperation and sense of being trapped, forever, in poverty.

Gideon lived in the luxurious world; she pretended she had even an inkling of what kind of privilege was like. Gideon owned famous works of art; she still kept her pasties in her underwear drawer.

"Can we talk about something else?" she asked.

His gaze roamed over her face, and she thought he might push, but he surprised her again by nodding. "Seen any good movies lately?"

"Not too many. I've been working long hours on the auction."

"We should go see that new murder mystery."

She shook her head. "Too dark. I like romantic comedies. That's what Andrew and I usually see."

"You do, huh?"

"Yeah. We usually agree on the same hunky actors."

"Oh, yeah."

Jacinda laughed at the less-than-excited expression on his face. "Mmm. Maybe not. How about TV shows?"

There they actually agreed on a few, and the conversation reminded her of the qualities she'd seen in him the night they'd met. She hadn't been attracted to only his smile, charm and gorgeous face. He'd listened when she talked. He was direct and opinionated, confident and understanding.

And hot. Don't forget very hot.

"What time are your dinner plans?"

"My—" She stopped, remembering suddenly that she'd told him she had previous plans to avoid having dinner with him. A lot of good *that* did. She'd hoped to avoid the intimacy of a restaurant, the implication of any kind of relationship. But they'd been pretty cozy for the past hour at the bar, and nobody looking at them would mistake them for strangers. The chemistry between them still existed. Maybe even stronger than before because they both knew how good they were together.

That idea should send her scrambling for cover. She was supposed to be remembering that impulsive decisions led nowhere productive. She was supposed to be telling herself her job was at risk. She was supposed to be firmly on the side of the auction house.

Instead, she wanted Gideon.

Maybe it was the stories of his adventures. Maybe it was the reminder of the daring, sexually aware woman she'd been the last time she'd seen Gideon. He forced her to remember that she used to be outgoing. She used to have *fun*.

These days she was always paranoid about doing or saying the right thing. She focused on advancing her career, on networking with guys instead of appreciating their smile or noticing the breadth of their shoulders in their expensive suits.

In fact, she couldn't remember the last date she'd been on. Why did doing her job well mean seriously neglecting her personal life?

She'd had relationships with a whopping *two* guys since leaving Vegas. There were a few itches that a woman needed to scratch every so often and so few men able to oblige.

At least not in the way she wanted.

Most of the guys she met either wanted one night of Playboy-quality sex—complete with toys and video cameras—or they wanted a wife and mother to their children as of yesterday. The typical guy who had partied and screwed around, and now he had the big corner office and important partnership. He wanted the picket fence in Connecticut, complete with a lovely, amiable wife, who'd give dinner parties and laugh at his boss's jokes.

A lot of women with her background would leap over tall buildings in a single bound in order to get security like that. But the idea of letting somebody else guide her emotional and financial future scared the crap out of Jacinda. The idea of being a trophy wife, spending her life doing charity work and playing tennis, made her want to dart into the speeding traffic down Fifth Avenue.

With Gideon, she knew the sex would satisfy—and then some. But could the sex stay simple and fun? Could she keep him away from her job, and her job away from her past? Sure, he was going to complicate life at work with his emerald ownership claims.

But she wasn't talking about a *relationship*. After his claims were either proven or discredited, he'd be gone again.

She'd already blurred the boundaries with him. Back in Vegas she'd slept with Gideon when any personal involvement with a customer could have gotten her fired. The temptation to do it again was palpable… Still, when he'd walked into her office today, she'd gone into a cold sweat worrying her past had caught up with her. Could she live with the constant threat of exposure?

He'd be at the office to launch his emerald claims whether they were involved or not. And maybe those discussions wouldn't be quite so hostile if—

"That's some pretty deep thinking going on," he said, leaning close and breaking in to her argument with herself. "You don't have dinner plans, do you?"

The no-strings-attached, itch-scratching moments with him were definitely numbered. The ownership issue would be resolved and Gideon would leave.

And she had a really sensitive spot just behind her ear....

She turned her head, relishing the heat of his stare, the interest and honesty in his eyes. "I do if you want to take me somewhere."

THEY DECIDED to stay at the restaurant.

Within a couple of minutes of speaking to the maître d', Gideon had arranged for an intimate table in the back corner, where they ordered shrimp and asparagus wraps, coconut soup and shrimp pad Thai.

Everything about tonight reminded him of why he'd been so attracted to her six years ago. Other than the obvious physical attributes—and those were certainly worth mentioning—she was witty, kind and smart as hell.

He loved watching her hair fall across her cheek when she leaned forward. He liked her directness and honesty—especially since he hadn't been so truthful with her. And every time her eyes sparkled with laughter, he felt an answering tug of pleasure in his groin.

With each moment in her presence, he wanted her more. And with each moment that passed he forgot his mission, why he'd sought her out in the first place.

Emerald? Who needed a stinking emerald?

"So what are your plans, Gideon Nash?" Jacinda asked, holding her wineglass as she leaned back in the booth and the waiter whisked away the plates. "Other than the emerald, why are you in New York?"

"My plans are to recover the emerald. That's the only reason I'm in the city."

"And say you get it. What then?"

"Off to the next adventure."

She snapped her fingers. "Like that."

"My bag is always packed, just like I told you in Vegas. That hasn't changed." He lowered his voice. "I didn't lie about everything."

"You just lied about the money."

He winced. Being reminded he'd been an ass wasn't exactly normal date conversation.

Is that what this is? A date?

If so, where was it going from here? He knew where he'd like it to go, but jumping into bed again was chemical and instinctive. And fun. Tempting. Wildly satisfying.

But was it wise?

"Your family is here," she said, breaking in to his thoughts. "You don't live here?"

He shrugged, feeling the familiar weight of family obligations and opinions on his shoulders. "I live on the road. But I do own a brownstone in Midtown. I'm staying there while I'm here. It won't be long."

She ran her finger around the rim of her crystal glass, her relaxed posture opposing the tension that had jumped between them. "Confident you'll get back the emerald?"

"It's mine," he said simply.

"Mmm. So you say."

"You think I'd try to swindle you?" He narrowed his eyes. "To take something that's not mine? You think I'd lie to benefit—" He stopped when her eyebrows rose into her hairline.

"Yourself?" She gave him a confident, half smile. "Especially since you've never lied before."

He bowed his head. No escaping that one. "I was a jerk before. I should have told you the truth. I apologize again. I didn't put any faith in you. Or in us. It's no wonder you didn't want to go away with me."

"When would you have told me?"

Laying his hands on the table, he linked his fingers. He felt ashamed and unsure, two emotions he rarely experienced. "I don't know. I hadn't thought that far ahead."

"I don't think either of us thought beyond the moment that weekend."

"A big part of the problem."

She nodded. "We jumped over several steps in the dating game."

He slid closer, then drew his finger down her thigh. "True. But fast isn't always bad." He grinned. "Not that I'm opposed to slow and easy."

Her eyes widened, then she smiled. "I remember."

"And I recall developing a taste for champagne that I hadn't had before."

"You licked it off nearly every inch of my body. I assumed you loved the stuff."

He slid his hand over her knee, then drew it up, along her thigh and under her skirt. "I loved the taste of it on your skin."

Her breathing hitched. She set her wineglass on the table.

His heart hammering, he leaned closer. His forehead brushed her hair as he spoke softly into her ear. "You have the softest skin."

"You think so?" she asked, her voice high and strained.

His pulse jumped. The wild attraction he still felt was reciprocated. He wasn't the only one veering way off his professional path and reliving their sensual history.

He glided his fingers up and down her thigh. Her skin heated beneath his touch. Her breathing quickened. He remembered those long, lean legs wrapped around his hips. He remembered them glistening with sweat, twitching in sensual need.

Drawing his hand higher on her leg, he moved closer to the juncture between her thighs. With the tip of his finger, he teased the edge of her panties. "I could make you forget your stress at work, even the conflict between us." He slid his finger into her warmth, finding the button that would send her soaring easily and quickly.

She gripped the edge of the table. "Gideon..."

"Is that a warning or encouragement?" He stroked his finger up, then down. He moved so slowly he hoped her eyes were crossed. He couldn't tell, of course, because she'd closed her lids.

To shut him out, or to better concentrate on the pleasure he was giving her?

The heat spilling off her body, pulsing against his fingers, had him holding his breath, anticipating her next sigh.

They were in a busy restaurant, staff and other customers just feet away, but that all fell away. There was only her. The woman he couldn't seem to forget. The woman he, again, couldn't resist.

"I think we should pick up where we left off," he said quietly in her ear.

She gasped, her thighs clenching around his hand. "Wh—where was that?"

"Naked and horizontal."

4

JACINDA'S EYES popped open. She clamped her thighs together, which only served to trap Gideon's hand against her bare flesh.

She ground her teeth as the tension building low in her belly jumped another notch.

Naked? Horizontal?

Who needed that? She was on the verge of orgasm with all her clothes on in a busy restaurant.

Not a good move—personally or professionally. Gideon was, no doubt, attempting to seduce the emerald out of her. Or at least persuade her to help him get it away from the documented owners.

She was nothing more to him.

Part of her knew giving in to the pleasure he could bring was impulsive, unethical and cheap. And part of her just didn't give a damn.

That was Jacy Powers talking.

She reminded the respectable Jacinda that it didn't do any good to run from the past. Old mistakes and experiences always found you just when you thought you'd moved, even risen above.

Great, now I'm referring to myself in the third person.

"Shall I continue?" Gideon's silky voice whispered in her ear.

"Certainly not here."

Oh, boy, now I'm talking like Jacinda and thinking like Jacy.

"My place?" he asked. "Or yours?"

She bit her lip. "Mine's closer."

He urged her chin around so they were face-to-face. "Is that an invitation?"

Trembling with need, doubt and anticipation, she nodded.

"I'll pay the check."

As he slid out of the booth, she nearly called him back—and not just because he'd moved his hand from between her legs. Surely sophisticated Manhattan career women didn't let guys feel them up in public, then invite them to their apartments for a hot, one-night stand they absolutely *knew* they'd regret in the morning.

If you knew you were making a mistake as you did something, shouldn't you stop yourself?

Apparently not, because when Gideon reappeared at the table and held out his hand, she took it and followed him out of the restaurant.

Was she drunk?

She rolled her head from side to side to check for dizziness.

When the world didn't spin and she continued to walk easily in her three-inch heels, she figured she'd passed that test. But was that a good thing?

She felt as if she were sleepwalking or dreaming, so she could explore what she wanted without consequences, because she'd wake up and come to her senses at any moment. But she didn't *want* to wake up. And she'd just have to pay the price for whatever came tomorrow. She'd spent years being practical and smart. For once, for just one night, she wanted to let go, she wanted to remember what it was like to be wild and free.

Gideon hailed a cab, and they climbed into the back-seat.

"Where to?" the cabbie asked.

Jacinda looked at Gideon. And, wow, he was something to look at. Piercing green eyes, silky-looking black hair, strong jaw.

Suddenly she realized her affliction, the judgment-robbing disease she'd come down with in the last few hours.

Gideonitis.

She was under the spell of Gideon Nash.

She mumbled her address while continuing to smile like a fool at the man next to her.

He angled his head. "Are you okay?"

See, he's sharp and intuitive as well as gorgeous. Clearly, he knows something's off about me.

"Ah, I'm not sure," she said.

"What can I—"

"Kiss me. I need you to kiss me."

"Now?"

Jacinda glanced at the rearview mirror and briefly met the interested cabbie's gaze. He'd no doubt seen and heard stranger things.

"Definitely," she said, her stomach shaking with renewed doubts.

Gideon leaned in, cupping her chin in his hand as his lips touched hers for the first time in six years.

His mouth captured hers with confidence, his tongue

sliding inside to taste and arouse. The electricity and power between them sparked to life with renewed energy. The cab disappeared, the city lights and the street noise fell away. She felt only the warm, spicy taste of Gideon.

She clenched the front of his shirt. His heart beat rapidly beneath her fist.

When he touched her everything seemed right and wonderful. Her doubts fell away, anticipation grew, desire rose. If she paused to think, she might change her mind about jumping into bed with Gideon.

"Better?" he asked softly against her mouth.

She sighed blissfully. "Much."

And she knew she didn't want to change her mind. She wanted to feel, to soar.

But she wanted those things on her terms.

She wanted to be safe from relationships that never seemed to go anywhere, or forced her to choose and compromise areas she didn't want to change. She knew her hesitancy for a real relationship was rooted from her years in uncertain poverty, then later cemented when she danced.

She didn't trust men.

Their smiles and their promises of security always faded, or turned out to be lies from the start. Her mother's succession of boyfriends had been a revolving door of hope and heartbreak, and Jacinda always swore she'd never fall into that trap. She'd be practical.

She'd rely only on herself.

So, while her friends would advise caution with Gideon, and Andrew would be jealous, she *knew* Gideon was simply safe. He wouldn't require a commitment or emotional attachment. He wouldn't promise things he had no intention or capability of delivering.

Tonight, she intended to have her cake, eat it and not count the calories.

As GIDEON HELPED Jacinda from the cab in front of her apartment building, he stared at the long, slender length of her legs.

His heart jumped. His erection swelled.

He paid the cabbie in a haze of need and expectation. He ignored his practical side—well, really it was a practical *section,* a very *small* section—telling him he and Jacinda were going too fast. Reminding him that spontaneous moves hadn't led anywhere productive last time.

Thankfully, the other ninety-five percent of him remembered the two nights of hot sex and told his practical section to pipe down ASAP.

Look into her eyes, not at her legs, his practical section insisted as they stepped into the elevator. *Doesn't something seem not quite right?*

Before that idea could take hold, Jacinda came to his rescue. She wrapped her arms around his neck and tangled her fingers in his hair. "I've wanted to do that all night."

He slid his arms around her waist. "Keep doing anything you like."

She kissed his throat, her hands gliding through his hair, her breasts brushing his chest. He closed his eyes to concentrate on the sensations flowing through his body, on the sexual friction they created.

How had he survived so long without touching her? Both the ache and the satisfaction were equally prized. No other woman had made him appreciate the journey to fulfillment more.

When the elevator doors opened, he spun Jacinda into the hall, keeping her tight against his body and hoping none of her neighbors were wandering around.

"What number?" he asked against her cheek.

"Seventeen twenty-one. To the right."

They moved in that direction, and as she unlocked her door, he grasped her waist, pulling her backside against his erection. He sucked in a quick breath of pain and pleasure. It was a sweet kind of torture to touch her, but not touch her completely.

He wanted to press her against the door, release himself from his jeans and slam his way to ecstasy.

Would this new, sophisticated Jacinda slap his face or hitch her legs around his hips and hold on for the ride? The fact that he couldn't anticipate her reaction when he thought he knew her well was both intriguing and frustrating.

Once she pushed open the door, she grabbed his hand and tugged him inside. He absorbed a brief glimpse of a sunken living room, ultramodern furniture in lots of silver and white and an excellent view of Central Park before she tugged him down a short hallway to her bedroom.

The room was awash in turquoise and green, reminding him of the Caribbean Sea. The sleek, almost sterile lines from the other room were gone, replaced by a wavy-patterned bedspread and delicate, sun-bleached seashells arranged in a crystal bowl on the nightstand.

He'd just caught a glimpse of a picture of Jacinda and a blond-haired man posing in the shallows of the ocean when her bra hit the carpeted floor.

"Are we—"

"We're getting naked," she said, planting her hands on her hips as his gaze took in her naked-to-the-waist lushness.

Sweat broke out on his brow. Dear heaven, he'd somehow forgotten how amazing her body was.

She angled her head. "It's better naked, don't you think?"

"Ah, it's pretty good no matter what."

She grinned. "True." She flopped back on the bed, her elegant skirt hitched halfway up her thighs.

And just like that, with her nearly naked, her eyes glittering and need clearly stamped on her face, he wanted to slow things way down.

He hadn't gone to Jacinda to charm his way into her bed—though that might have been a secondary thought after he'd acquired the emerald. He'd hoped their past would have established a familiarity and sense of trust that he wouldn't have gotten from another auction house staff member.

He knew Jacinda. He knew she was honest and determined, smart and professional. He admired her guts, ambition and resourcefulness to use all the assets she possessed to get what she wanted—namely, her body *and* her brains.

He hadn't counted on her being ashamed of her past, though why the hell that hadn't occurred to him was, at the moment, a complete mystery of idiocy.

In retrospect, he wished he could have marched into a stranger's office, said the name *Sophia Graystone* and waited for them to bow at his feet. As he watched Jacinda crook her finger toward him, he realized he'd tangled his past and present, his professional and personal lives far too intimately.

Jump her! his body urged. *Who cares how complicated things get?*

He waited, for just a second, for his practical section to argue.

Silence.

Grinning, he dropped to the bed beside her. He laid on his side and drew his finger down the center of her bare chest. "We don't have to be in a hurry, do we?"

She rolled over on top of him, straddling his hips. "Sure we do."

"That works, too," he said, reaching for the zipper at the back of her skirt as she shoved his T-shirt up.

When she'd bared his chest, she leaned down...kissed his neck, then quickly moved to his nipples. She flicked her tongue across each one in turn, shooting flames of pleasure to his groin.

All he could manage to do was grip the comforter in his fists and arch into her touch.

Being the determined, multitasking woman she was, she managed to release the buttons on his jeans, even as her mouth and tongue continued their exploration of his chest. She rendered him helpless and needy so quickly. His senses were bombarded by her, the feel of her hot, bare skin against his, her breasts brushing his chest, her palms skimming his sides.

Her scent washed over him, like coconut milk, but also slightly tangy like the sea. The only sounds in the room were the combination of their breathing and the occasional horn from the street outside. But he imagined hearing the crashing ocean waves. He'd like to see her in the sand, digging—

His breath froze in his chest as she released his erection, cupping him and running her hand up and down its rigid length. His heart pounded like a chugging freight train.

"Oh, man."

Jacinda's face hovered above his. "I think I remember where this goes."

He croaked out a chuckle. He wasn't going to last long if she kept doing that. "If you forget, I'll remind you."

She released him suddenly, and he sat up. "Hey, where—"

She'd scooted to the bedside table, where she pulled out a foil-wrapped condom. She tossed it to him, then wriggled her way out of her skirt and panties.

He stopped himself from asking her to move slower, to draw out the striptease. But since his erection was throbbing impatiently, he rolled on the protection.

The moment she was naked, he grabbed her arm and tugged her onto her back, then positioned himself between her legs.

"My stamina isn't great. I've spent the last four months in the Andes."

"No sex in four months?"

"None."

She smiled. "I'll be happy to get you back in the swing of things." She grabbed his hips and pulled him deep inside her.

His breath released in a whoosh, and he lay still for a moment, absorbing the pulsing beats of their hearts, relishing the heat and closeness.

But his body didn't want quiet reflection, it wanted to

move. He lifted his hips, then sank deeper inside, earning a throaty moan of approval from Jacinda. He continued moving with as much control as he could manage, desperately holding back the urge to quicken his thrusts, to drive toward completion without any finesse or gentleness.

Then she wrapped her legs around his hips and arched her back, her eyes fluttering closed, her breathing growing shallow and labored. Her obvious pleasure increased his own. He longed to draw out both of their satisfaction, but his muscles were tight from holding back. His body was screaming at him.

He moved his hands underneath her, shifting the angle of her hips, penetrating in a different way, a way he distinctly remembered her enjoying quite a bit.

Her breath caught. Her fingers dug into his sides. Her neck arched.

In turn, sensing her orgasm approaching, he moved faster, harder, the beginnings of his climax clenching at the base of his spine.

She moaned and tightened her thighs around him. Her body glistened with sweat as their bodies moved together, the fire between them growing hotter, stronger.

As her inner walls pulsed around him and her body jerked, his own orgasm shot through him, and he knew his intense satisfaction was different than it had been in a long, long time.

Damn, he'd missed her. He'd really missed her.

JACINDA LAID HER PALM against Gideon's damp shoulder. "I can't breathe," she gasped.

"Mmm. Sorry." He obligingly rolled off her, though he

didn't release her. She wound up sprawled across his chest, their legs still tangled, their hearts still beating as one.

She swallowed a burst of panic at the cozy position. Weren't men the ones who either jumped out of bed or fell asleep after sex, thereby avoiding any sort of meaningful, what-did-we-just-share conversation?

Shouldn't *he* be the one itching to get out of bed, get into his clothes and get out? Why did the intimacy make *her* itchy and panicky?

Ah, because you have serious trust issues?

Oh, yeah, there was that.

She rolled off him and off the bed with as much grace and nonchalance as she could manage naked. "I'm getting some water. You want some?"

He grunted.

Please don't let him fall asleep, please don't let him fall asleep, she prayed silently as she walked into the bathroom and wondered if she could be so nonchalant about causing a really loud disturbance that would startle Gideon out of his stupor.

In front of the sink, she avoided her reflection and splashed cold water on her face. With the itch of desire satiated, she knew reality would return soon enough. She'd face herself—and her choices—then.

She smoothed a bit of her coconut-scented lotion on her arms, chest and legs, then slipped into the cushy white robe that hung on the back of the door.

Maybe when she returned to the bedroom, he'd be dressed and alert. She could kiss his cheek, then send him on his way.

When she opened the door, she noticed him sitting on the edge of the bed. He was wearing his jeans.

Halfway there.

She approached him cautiously, uncertain of his mood. Surely he wasn't going to throw out some flowery speech, or declare she was the best lover ever, even though they *were* pretty darn terrific together, and she *definitely* didn't want the opposite reaction—asking where the remote was so he could catch the last few minutes of sports news on TV. That had certainly happened before, too.

He did neither. Instead, he watched her out of eyes as fathomless and beautiful as the emerald. In that moment, she realized the emerald's unusual color, both blue and green, would be like combining her and Gideon's eye colors.

She refused to get all dramatic and act as if she was sleeping with the enemy, but she *had* taken a risk. If Gideon decided to play nasty about the ownership of the gem, he could expose their relationship—both past and present. He could tell her boss about her years in Vegas, that she had absolutely no business socializing and working with the auction house's clientele, that she was pretending to be part of a world she couldn't really ever inhabit.

To her relief, he smiled and extended his hand, which she took, allowing him to pull her into his lap.

Touching him, one arm slung around his neck, his skin warming hers, she managed to let go of the proverbial breath she'd been holding.

This was Gideon. Fun, impulsive, adventurous. She didn't have to worry about awkward, deep conversations, or questions such as "Where do we go from here?" This was just what she needed. Easy and predictable.

"How about dessert?" he asked.

She raised her eyebrows. "We didn't just have it?"

"It was a start."

A start?

She held on as he scooped her into his arms and strode from the room. He walked past the sunken living room to the kitchen and set her on one of the high stools beside the long, curving bar separating the two rooms.

He headed to the fridge, where Jacinda knew he wouldn't find anything more appetizing than yogurt or leftover Chinese takeout. She liked to cook on weekends when she could, but the upcoming auction had consumed even that little time off.

"You have any apples?" he asked, bent in half at the open fridge door.

"Maybe. Try the bottom bin."

He retrieved two red apples, put them on the counter, then rummaged through the cabinets until he found the pantry. There, he pulled out a jar of peanut butter. After locating a knife and cutting board, he rounded the bar and set the supplies between them.

"Apples and peanut butter?" she asked, glancing down. "Dessert?"

"Good for you," he said, handing her a freshly cut slice smeared with PB. "Lots of energy."

Their gazes met for a brief second, and they shared a laugh.

Easy. Predictable. Even comfortable.

"Nice apartment," he said, glancing around a little too casually.

She'd wondered when he was going to ask her about her tony address and designer furnishings. She was paid well, but this place had probably cost a couple million at least.

"It's not really mine. I'm leasing it from a friend who's

traveling. In exchange for looking after his cats, I get cheap rent." She cast her gaze toward the windows and sparkling sky beyond. "And a great view."

"Cats? What cats?"

"They'll pop out eventually." She grinned. "They *love* peanut butter."

"Your landlord, is that the guy in the picture on your nightstand?"

"The picture on my…" She paused, remembering Gideon was a hunter, a trained observer and fact gatherer. "That's Andrew."

"Your assistant?"

"Yeah. You met him, remember?" She waved her hand. "He bleached his hair nearly white before we went to St. Croix last winter with a group of friends. I grew up never having seen the ocean, so I go to the beach whenever I can get away."

He nodded as if he ran in to people who'd never been to the coast all the time, which, of course, he didn't. "How old were you the first time?"

"Twenty-four. When I moved here," she added in case he missed the point.

"My family owns a place in Bermuda. I'll take you sometime."

"Sure," she said casually, with the understanding that it was an empty invitation, one she'd heard from people many times over the last few years. "I could use a tan after being cooped up at the office the last few months."

"How about next—" He stopped, his hand clenching into a fist when a cat jumped onto the bar.

Jacinda was briefly distracted by the bunching of Gideon's forearms and shoulder muscles, so it took her a moment to notice not only Lochy, but Ralph, who'd jumped onto the bar next to his companion. "Told you they love peanut butter," she said when Gideon remained frozen, staring at the cats.

"That is the strangest pair of animals I've ever seen."

"Yep." Jacinda scooped out a dollop of peanut butter with a spoon and held it out to Ralph. "Ralph here is a stray. He's blind in one eye and has a limp. He was in a serious fight at some point and lost several tufts of hair. They've never grown back at the right length or thickness, even for a shorthair. His dark yellow fur is natural. He's not dirty, even though he always looks like he needs a bath."

"And what about him?" Gideon asked, pointing at Ralph's regal-looking companion.

"That's Lochy. Put a scoop of peanut butter on your finger and hold it out. He won't eat it from a spoon." When Gideon hesitated, she added, "Go on. He'd never bite another purebred."

A little leery, Gideon held out a peanut butter–covered finger, and after giving him a brief once-over, Lochy began to lick delicately at the treat. "He looks like one of those high-dollar Persians who eat out of crystal dishes."

"Crystal dish, yes. Persian, no. That is Lochinvas Fortisecue, a blue-point Himalayan with six national championships and a direct descendant of Pasturelli's Camenbert, the most prized purebred show cat in all of North America."

"All that for a black-and-white cat—" Gideon leaned closer "—with kinda scary blue eyes?"

"Trust me, in the feline world he's a god."

"How did your friend wind up with both of them?"

"He has a sense of irony and charity." Her voice softened. "Look what he's done for me."

Gideon's jaw tightened. "Some sugar daddy. I would have thought you were too independent for that lifestyle."

Patrick was a mentor, not a lover, and she was saddened to learn Gideon had immediately jumped to the most lascivious explanation, the obvious one for a former exotic dancer. She had thought better of him.

She slid off the bar stool. "Why don't you get the rest of your clothes? I'll clean up in here."

He grabbed her hand as she started to round the bar. "I'm sorry. That was a jackass thing to say."

Still surprised by the intensity of her disappointment, she didn't look at him. "I have to get up early, as I imagine you do."

"Look at me, please."

She finally turned her head to look at him and tried to make herself feel nothing. His opinion of her shouldn't be surprising. Many people over the years had certainly thought casino waitress or dancer was one small step from prostitution.

Most of them just didn't say so to her face.

"I'm sorry," he said quietly.

"I left my shame behind in Vegas, too. I don't need your judgment."

"I'm not judging you."

She smiled coldly. "Aren't you?"

He sighed. "Damn it, Jacy, I—"

"My name is *Jacinda*," she said as she jerked her hand away.

She'd taken only two steps when he wrapped his arms

around her from behind. "Are you going to kick me out now, Jacinda?"

The intimacy of their positions and the soft steel in his voice made her knees weak. She tried to remind herself that they weren't friends, but simply old acquaintances, reuniting for one night of fun.

But with a single touch he reminded her their relationship was much more complicated.

There were moments when his eyes seemed to promise more than sex, when his words touched her and made her heart flutter. There had been moments all evening when she'd wondered if she wanted more. With him.

With anybody.

She shoved those thoughts aside. She wanted a hot night; she'd gotten one. That was it. Right? "You remind me of a past I want to forget. I don't want to be who I was."

"I liked who you were. I like who you are. Can't it be that simple?"

"I don't see how."

She'd thought she could somehow separate who she was during the day with who she wanted to be at night, with Gideon, but everything was too tangled up, too quickly.

She wanted him gone; she wanted him here. The opposing feelings were unnerving. He knew her too well, both body and mind. She trusted him with her body, but every other part of her was holding back. "I don't like you knowing about my past."

"I was jealous," he said at the same time.

She glanced over her shoulder at him. "What?"

"When I saw the beach picture in your bedroom."

"I told you. That's An—"

"I know." He stroked her cheek with the back of his hand. "I know that now."

"Why are you telling me this?"

"You admitted something personal. I'm reciprocating."

Oh, hell, they were *sharing*. They were having a meaningful conversation and expressing significant emotions.

Why couldn't it just be easy and fun? What happened to a simple release of tension? What happened to sex for the hell of it? The whole idea of something deeper, something closer, was scary and intimidating.

"This is different from last time," she said. "It feels very different."

"For me, too."

"I don't like it."

He smiled, then leaned closer and cupped her jaw, his lips a mere inch from hers. "I'm not completely sure I do, either."

"What are we going to do about it?"

"What we always do—go with the moment."

5

GIDEON COVERED Jacinda's mouth with his own, relishing her warmth and sweet, peanut-buttery taste.

He slid his tongue slowly, carefully past her lips, which somehow felt more intimate than when they'd been naked on her bed.

Why did everything feel different this time? Why did words and actions have more weight? Why did emotions run so deeply?

He knew very little, except he wanted her more than ever. He must have been crazy to think he could approach her about the emerald without putting his hands all over her. He'd lost something important in Vegas, and it wasn't gold, silver or gems.

He didn't want her to run again, and he didn't want to walk away. He was going to find out what they could be together *and* he was going to get his emerald.

Pulling back, he stared into her desire-filled eyes and debated whether he should coax her back to bed, or give her space to realize tonight meant more than either of them had intended.

Leave her wanting more, his practical section advised.

She needed space, and he had boxes of evidence relating to the emerald to go through. "I'm going to get dressed," he said.

Not waiting for her response, he strode to her bedroom, tugged on his shirt, then put on his socks and shoes. When he returned to the other room, she was still standing next to the bar, stroking the odd pair of cats under their chins.

"So, I'll see you in the morning, right?"

"In the morning?"

"So I can meet with you and your boss about the emerald. What time is good?"

"Meet with my—" She approached him, glaring through narrowed eyes—a lot like the cats. "I don't set up business meetings while wearing my bathrobe."

"How about I call you in the morning?"

"No."

"No? The auction is less than a week away, when do you suggest I make an appointment?"

"Never."

Something was really, really wrong here, and he'd be damned if he could figure out what.

"I guess the sex was just part one of your negotiations," she went on. "Clever, actually."

"Sex? No. I have receipts, signed witness testimony and pawnshop coupons."

"You sure you didn't sleep with me to soften me up, so that I'd put in a good word for you with my boss?"

What was with her? Their relationship didn't have anything to do with the emerald. "No, of course not."

"I don't believe you."

"You what? Jacinda, this is—"

"Ridiculous? Crazy?" She took another step toward him, her expression so fierce, he actually retreated. "You bet your ass it is. I had to be out of my mind, inviting you here. You couldn't even wait until the sheets got cold before working things around to that damn stone."

"I was completely up-front with you about why I came to New York."

Still advancing on him, she looked ready to spit nails. "Were you?"

If she called him a liar one more damn time... However, he now recognized his timing in talking about the meeting had been ill-advised. "Yes. Tonight has nothing to with my claims on the emerald. I'd appreciate if you were at the meeting, of course, but—"

"I don't want you anywhere near my or my boss's office. This is my first auction. This is my chance to prove myself, and you're going to ruin everything."

She'd managed to back him against the door, and he used his leverage to lay his hands on her shoulders. "I'm sorry to cause you trouble about the auction. Truly I am. But you can just quietly pull the stone off the docket. It's not like I'm going to take an ad out in the newspaper about all this."

She shrugged off his touch and turned away. "Get out."

"Jacinda, please."

"It was fun," she said without turning around, "but it's time for you to go."

He didn't expect the sharp pain to his chest. Her cold dismissal reminded him that whatever he felt about them, it obviously didn't go beyond a physical attraction for her.

"I'll see you tomorrow," he said quietly, then slipped out the door.

"Ms. Barrett," Sherman Pascowitz said with a stern look in his beady eyes, "in light of this information, I see no choice but to pull the Veros emerald from the auction."

Jacinda's only physical reaction was her knuckles whitening where her hands lay linked in her lap, but Gideon knew she was furious.

At him as much as, if not more than, at her boss.

That morning, Gideon had not only packed up his box containing nearly every printed document and photograph he possessed about the emerald, but he'd also put together a slide show presentation with his digitally stored backup files.

If he'd had Jacinda on his side, he wouldn't have had to pull out all the stops. Instead he'd researched her boss last night—since he'd been too worked up to sleep—and figured the guy for somebody to be impressed by bells and whistles.

For all the preparation, this was still one of the tensest meetings Gideon had ever attended.

Poor Pascowitz clearly didn't want a scandal to pull the emerald from the sale, but he was also terrified of offending Sophia Graystone. Jacinda was obviously—at least to him—furious at Gideon for arranging the impromptu meeting with the auction house director, and her mood hadn't improved as Gideon had presented his case.

She couldn't deny how compelling his proof was or how well he'd organized his data—something he was sure Jacinda hadn't anticipated from her aimless adventurer.

"While I agree Mr. Nash's evidence is *interesting*," she began in a calm, controlled, but still somehow doubtful tone, "there is still nothing definitive. The pictures are simply too old, and the appraisal too vague."

Pascowitz mulled over this.

Confident and oddly enjoying the chance to spar with Jacinda, Gideon leaned back in his chair. "While it's true that jewelry appraisal has come a long way in sixty years,

I'd like to point out that I have the statement from the pawnshop owner, whose grandfather acquired the emerald—which was set in a necklace at the time—just three weeks after my grandmother left England."

"That is certainly strong evidence, Ms. Barrett," Pascowitz, who still seemed uncertain which side he should be on, said.

"There's no police report," Jacinda said.

Anticipating the question and regretful he had to lie, Gideon shrugged. "Unfortunately, those records were misplaced over the years."

"The Veros family are valuable clients," Jacinda said, "whose reputation could be damaged by any suggestion they acquired the stone by less than ethical means. If the gem is withdrawn this close to the auction, surely speculation will follow."

Pascowitz frowned, stroking his weak chin. "True."

As if sensing an advantage, Jacinda pounced. "I think we should table the discussion. At least until Monday, sir."

"It wouldn't do to make a rash decision," Pascowitz muttered. "Pulling any items from the auction means notifying the board of directors."

Gideon could almost hear the rest of his thought—*And it is Friday afternoon...*

Gideon knew when a deal was going sour, and he wasn't about to let that happen here. It was time to pull out those Graystone family manners that tended to get moldy from lack of use.

Rising, he held out his hand to Pascowitz. "I appreciate your time, sir. Please let me know when you've reached a decision. Time is critical, as I'm sure you realize."

Pascowitz shook his hand, then as Gideon turned to

leave, the director rushed around his desk, his face anxious. "There is a great deal to consider, Mr. Nash, but please assure your grandmother that Callibro's will handle the matter with the utmost care and discretion."

Though Pascowitz was a pompous coward and certain to spend the weekend searching for a way to keep both the Graystone and Veros families happy, he knew how to kiss ass like a champ.

"I'm sure you will."

"I'll see him out, sir," Jacinda said, following Gideon to the door.

They walked silently down the hall, then turned the corner and headed to Jacinda's office. As much as Gideon tried to remind himself that not only had Jacinda not gone to bat for him, but she'd also actually argued *against* him, he still couldn't resist watching her hips twitch as she moved.

Is it possible to keep your mind off sex for one minute? his practical section asked, annoyed.

Apparently not, since the moment he closed Jacinda's office door behind him, his gaze raked her, imagining the lingerie she wore and wondering how quickly he could see it, before taking it all off.

"You *bribed* my boss," Jacinda said, obviously referring to the little "donation" he'd made to the auction house as an enticement for Pascowitz to see him.

"We didn't really need that candlestick in the dining room."

"You *bribed* my boss."

"I'm assuming you think that was wrong."

She turned away, then quickly faced him again. "I'm going to get fired."

He moved toward her. "You're going to get fired because I bribed your boss? He didn't even accept my claim. I'm not getting the emerald." *Not yet, anyway.*

"You will," she said, her eyes narrowed.

He hadn't anticipated this reaction. The emerald was one damn piece in her impressive auction collection. Who'd really miss it? She would still make a success out of the event.

"This is not my fault," he pointed out calmly, despite his growing temper and her obvious annoyance and disappointment. "Somebody *stole* that emerald from my grandmother. I'm simply getting it back."

Her eyes were like blue chips of ice. "You're defending your claim. I'm defending mine."

There was so much more to this than a business disagreement. But wasn't he the one who'd told her last night that the emerald had nothing to do with their relationship?

What an idiot he'd been.

"I'm not trying to complicate things for you," he said, knowing as he spoke that it was a weak defense.

"Too late. Who do you think Pascowitz is going to blame for all this? He won't accept responsibility himself, I can assure you. Then if he ever finds out about my past, he and the board will toss me aside faster than I can blink."

Personally he thought she greatly underestimated people's acceptance of her life—none of which was illegal—before she'd arrived in New York. Managers needed competent, hard-working people who didn't steal from their company. Who the hell cared about anybody's private life anymore?

But he knew she wasn't ready to hear that. "Who's going to tell him about your past?" he asked her instead.

"Nobody has to. Your presence here is enough."

That thinking was so incredibly paranoid he didn't know how to respond. He hung his head. Clearly, veering into the personal stuff was a bad idea. "Hell."

"And don't you think the Veros family will go to the press when they realize their claim to a two-million-dollar emerald has been questioned? This thing is going to hit the *Post* the second Pascowitz pulls the emerald off the list."

"I doubt they will. They won't be interested in aligning themselves with a theft, even an old one."

"But if they do—"

"Maybe they will." He sliced his hand through the air. As much as he desired her, she frustrated him to an equal level. "I can't do anything about that. But as an ethical businesswoman, in light of all the evidence I presented today, don't you think the emerald should be pulled from the auction? Don't you think I have a case?"

She braced her hands on her desk, looking as though she'd rather throw something at him. "Maybe it should be pulled. But I'm looking out for myself in this deal." She paused, giving him a pointed look. "Just like everybody else."

"I'm getting that gem back for my family's honor. It isn't a damn trophy."

Her tone was mocking. "Isn't it?"

AFTER SULKING half the night before and most of the day, Gideon paced his brownstone Saturday afternoon.

He was angry, frustrated and hurt.

And that damn green stone was the least of his problems.

Would that be the stone your grandmother doesn't

even want to discuss, *much less have hanging around her neck again?*

So maybe he had some minor details to work out on that front. But that was nothing compared to his personal issues.

He hadn't anticipated his emotions getting tangled up so thoroughly, so quickly. But they had.

His anger at Jacinda didn't stem from a logical, detached place. Jacinda, his lover, the woman he could never quite forget, was opposing his claim on a family heirloom to further her career.

He felt physically sick at the idea.

So he was pacing, trying to find a way to convince her that he wasn't out to hurt her or get her fired, that instead he wanted to discover how deep this connection between them went. If he told her that, of course, she'd run the other way.

Then again, if he could harness his anger and frustration with her, *he* could just walk away.

He dismissed that idea immediately. He *couldn't* walk away.

Part of him recognized the intriguing challenge he had in trying to change her opinion of him. She was wary of everybody, him in particular. She didn't think much of his character. Yesterday, hadn't she accused him of going after the emerald as a trophy? She might even consider herself a different kind of trophy.

Fortunately—or unfortunately, depending on which side you stood on—he didn't think of her that way at all. And he wasn't simply drawn to the challenge of winning her. No, he wanted her smile and her touch. He wanted her eyes to light up at the sight of him. He wanted to heal her resentment of the past. He wanted to see her accept herself—in every way.

So, for better or worse, he was sticking with his pursuit. And that meant he had to find a way to get past her wall of resentment and mistrust.

What assets did he have?

His charm and obvious sexual prowess, which Jacinda enjoyed but didn't seem particularly dazzled by. His sense of fun and adventure, which Jacinda seemed to enjoy in the bedroom, but nowhere else. His money, power and influence, which Jacinda seemed to care less about.

He could cook. Thanks to an Italian buddy, he could make a mean spaghetti sauce.

He paused in his pacing. Dinner had merit.

Women had chased men for centuries by appealing to their stomachs. Surely, in the twenty-first century, that logic could work the other way around.

He'd been in her apartment, after all, and had seen her selection of celery, old Chinese food, coffee and peanut butter. She *needed* a culinary upgrade.

He jumped in the shower, deciding he'd also rent a DVD, then do his shopping and just show up on Jacinda's doorstep. If he called her, she'd probably hang up on him. Or at the very least, say no to his offer. So no opportunity for refusal. And if she wasn't alone when he got to her apartment...

Well, he'd have to think fast.

That practical section of his brain cautioned him about pushing too hard for something more long-term with her when he knew he'd eventually launch his next quest for treasure. That certainly would strain the connection with Jacinda. Would they have established a tight enough relationship to survive months of separation?

Maybe you ought to get a second date before you start planning the future.

If there *was* a future, maybe he could actually convince her to come with him this time.

She'd be a great companion for his adventures, and they'd have a blast together. Her sharp mind and honed cynicism would serve them well in discerning frauds and legitimate leads. He could picture them trolling through the street markets in Bangladesh, or charming and bribing information out of a South Seas islander.

But searching on his own had served him well for many years. Could he really travel with somebody else? Especially a somebody else he wanted naked at every opportunity? Could he accomplish his goals and still have a serious relationship? Did he even *want* a serious relationship?

Asking somebody to travel to the far reaches of the earth with you is a pretty serious relationship.

And he was getting ahead of himself. Again. Grovel, have second date, then think about the future.

Just before six, he headed out to the market for the dinner ingredients, then moved on to Jacinda's apartment.

Correction, her *friend's* apartment.

Patrick O'Leary—millionaire software developer, semiretired, world traveler, respected animal-rights philanthropist, owner of one of the most famous cats on the planet.

Weird? Yes.

With a little more digging, Gideon had discovered the sixty-three-year-old O'Leary was spending the summer at his villa in the south of France, and he and Jacinda were close friends, not lovers.

At least Gideon had already apologized for that screwup.

Supplies for the perfect suck-up meal in hand, he fought to breathe normally and knocked on Jacinda's door.

She opened the door moments later and stood in the opening, scowling at him. "What are you doing here?"

Dressed in worn jeans and a pale pink T-shirt, with her hair in a ponytail, she looked beautiful—but certainly not expecting company. *One hurdle complete...*

He smiled brightly. "I'm here to make you dinner."

"What for?"

"To eat. Can I come in?"

Saying nothing, she stepped back and allowed him to enter.

I'm inside. That's hurdle number two.

"Did you take the day off?" he asked, heading toward the kitchen to set the bags on the counter.

She followed him. "I painted my toenails."

He glanced down to note their bright pink color and smiled. "You took off the whole day? You didn't go in to your office at all?"

"I talked to Andrew on the phone twice." She crossed her arms over her chest. "Gideon, do you remember we're standing on opposite sides of this emerald thing? Do you remember we argued yesterday?"

He held up a bottle of champagne wrapped in a bag of ice. "I remember. Champagne?"

"I'm still angry at you," she said slowly, as if he'd misunderstood her scowling expression and frosty glare.

"Well, I promise to get you only a bit tipsy." He slid one arm around her waist. "Just enough so I can take advantage of you."

She wriggled out of his arms. Good thing he hadn't anticipated seducing her quite that easily.

"I'm not pulling the emerald from the auction unless my boss forces me to. Are you willing to give up your claim on it?"

He was well aware he couldn't keep the emerald and their relationship in completely separate camps, but he was hoping they could find a way to meet in the middle. At the moment, though, his only goal was to reestablish their physical bond. "No."

"Then I don't see what we have to talk about."

"Who said we were going to talk?"

He searched the cabinets for glasses. When he found them, he popped the cork, then poured two flutes full of the bubbly. He extended one toward Jacinda.

She simply glared at him. "I'm not sleeping with you, either."

"Who said anything about sleeping?"

She snatched the glass from his hand and took a gulp. "You are the most annoying, aggravating, presumptuous man I've ever met."

"That's not much of a toast. If we're going to work through our relationship, you're going to have to be a little more cheerful."

"We don't have a relationship. I'm using you for sex."

He was disappointed by her answer, of course, but not really surprised. At least she'd referred to their sex life in the present tense. "You want to get naked now, or after dinner?"

Her jaw dropped. "Neither. I just told you—"

"You said no talking and no sleeping."

"I know, but—"

"You said you were using me for sex. You don't want to get naked for sex?"

"Just cook," she said, spinning away and heading toward the sofa, where she plopped down and sipped her champagne.

"Okay," he said easily. "How do you feel about—"

"And no talking."

He whistled.

She muttered. "Crazy man, showing up here, uninvited." She shook her head. "Cooking, champagne. What's he up to?"

Though it would be nice to have a date who was relaxed and flirty, instead of one who scowled at him and displayed her wariness like a badge of honor, he comforted himself with the knowledge that she hadn't thrown him out. And she'd admitted their chemistry.

Though she hadn't seemed too happy about it.

Vowing to stay optimistic and harboring dreams of heavy breathing and nakedness, he continued to whistle as he put the spaghetti sauce ingredients together.

After a while, he noticed she'd stopped muttering, had turned on the couch and was watching him over the back.

"More champagne?" he asked, walking toward her with the bottle.

"Sure." She held out her glass. Her gaze met his for a moment before she resumed her scowl and looked away. "That smells pretty good. Pasta sauce?"

"With a bit of Italian ground sausage. A family specialty."

"Whose family?"

"A friend of mine's. Are you through being angry at me?"

Her gaze flicked to his, and while she was clearly still not happy with him, her eyes had lost their coldness. "You shouldn't have contacted my boss."

"There, I'm afraid I'll have to disagree."

"Fine. You should be just as angry at me, you know. I'm not supporting you."

"I'm definitely disappointed, but I understand your reasons."

"You do?"

"Your job is the most important thing in your life. You don't want to jeopardize it."

Her face flushed as if she were embarrassed, but she nodded.

"Let's forget about the emerald—at least until Monday. I'm not going to be in town long, and I want to spend my time with you." He leaned down, cupping her jaw and brushing his lips across her cheek. He was playing to her desires of no-attachment sex, even as he fostered much bigger dreams. Foolish, probably. "Let me feed you... pleasure you."

"I'm not forgiving you," she said in a breathless voice.

"I know."

"I'm using you for sex."

"You said that already."

She leaned back and now she was smiling. "Just reminding you. You have a tendency to make up the rules as you go along, Gideon Nash."

He laughed. "Do I?"

6

DURING DINNER, he followed her lead and carefully avoided any meaningful discussion—of the emerald or their relationship—based-on-sex-only. They settled into innuendo and flirting, empty and meaningless. Just like six years ago.

And wasn't that what she wanted?

Thankfully, he said nothing to disturb the peace and played his part as the carefree adventurer, while she was silently grateful and amazed he'd sought her out tonight.

He couldn't be that hard up for bedmates. Why had he come? Why had he charmed her and coddled her? She had to be way more trouble than she was worth.

But full of pasta and garlic bread, she just didn't have the energy to examine his motives.

After they cleaned the dishes, she walked into the living room and turned on the stereo. Soft jazz glided from the speakers, filling the room with a quiet intimacy and layer of tension.

What now? the notes seemed to ask.

Gideon approached her from behind. "You want to dance?"

She whirled, her heart pounded. "Look, I don't—" She stopped and shook her head, smiling slightly. "Not *for* you. You mean *with* you. Sure."

He wrapped his hands around her wrists, then looped her arms around his neck. "I know you don't dance for people anymore," he said against her temple.

She tucked her head beneath his chin. "I know."

"I'm tiptoeing here."

"Don't. It's fine. It's just because I'm with you that the dancing thing caught me off guard."

He stroked her back. "I get it. I'm special."

She kissed his neck. "Mmm. Sure."

"However…if you wanted to roll your hips in slow, methodic circles, and if some piece of clothing happened to hit the floor…"

She laughed. "You're a pervert."

"*Ahem.* I'm a man."

"Exactly."

He pulled her closer, and they swayed to the music for about half a song, the wine and a full stomach adding to the sense of easy comfort. Then the heat and sensual tension that always flowed between them rumbled back to life. The desire that never seemed sated rolled through her veins like a river, an ache unfilled, an itch that constantly needed to be scratched.

His hands moved up and down her back, not in comfort, but in a massaging, arousing motion. His first touch to her bare skin was a kiss beneath her ear. Her breath caught, then released on a deep sigh, and her longing to possess him raged like a forest fire.

Instant. Hot. Wild.

He traced his hands beneath her T-shirt, his palms skimming her waist, the heat of his hand warming her. In a smooth motion, he pulled the shirt over her head, then dropped it on the floor. She felt free and uninhibited with him as no one else before.

She could be wild with him at night, and still be respectable at the office during the day. She could share her body, but protect her dreams, mind or goals.

It was perfect.

He kissed her neck and shoulders, his mouth lingering with gentle, but persistent arousal. Then he trailed his lips down her stomach, his tongue's path teasing and exciting. She arched her back and braced her hands on his shoulders as he knelt in front of her.

Continuing to place openmouthed kisses on her, he undid the button and zipper, then pushed the jeans over her hips, down her thighs and calves. She knew a bare scrap of bright yellow panties was now the only barrier to the essence of her body.

When he slid his finger beneath the elastic edge, Jacinda's knees nearly buckled. She was already hot for him, of course, already wet and dangling on the edge of orgasm.

Why was he the one who could do this so effortlessly? Why did one stroke of his finger make her clench her teeth and fight the urge to beg for more?

His finger entered her, stroking rhythmically, arousing her even further. His breath was hot against the lower part of her abdomen, and she dug her fingers into the muscles of his shoulders, silently asking for him to taste her, to end the sweet torture.

Then start all over again.

With one smooth move, she got her wish. He maneuvered her panties down her legs and left them to pool on the floor with her jeans. He didn't hesitate to dip his tongue into the flesh exposed.

Her head fell backward as his lips and teeth and tongue found just the right spot, the right rhythm and pressure to send her spiraling upward. Her climax rushed over her sooner than she expected, pulsing with marvelous energy, turning her muscles to liquid.

She would have collapsed on top of him if he hadn't supported her, then swung her into his arms. Depositing her on the sofa, he stroked her stomach lightly as her breathing slowed.

When she opened her eyes, she found herself naked and him fully dressed. She smiled, knowing she had to fix that ASAP.

She lifted off his T-shirt, exposing his leanly muscled chest, then tugged him against her, their bare skin connecting while her heart rate shot skyward again. Satisfying one urge didn't seem to sate her need for more.

With his help, she stripped the rest of his clothes off and pressed him back onto the sofa. She wrapped her hand around his erection as she placed kisses across his chest and stomach.

He groaned and angled his hips toward her, and she obligingly pumped her hand up, then down. His hardness pulsed against her palm, and a returning set of quivers slid down her spine, tightening the coil of desire deep inside her again.

She saw no reason not to return the favor he'd bestowed on her, so she slid farther down, replacing her hand with her mouth, taking him inside her, revving up his hunger.

As his hands brushed over the top of her head in silent approval, she relaxed her throat to take in more of him. This was not an act she'd performed on him before.

Her own body moaned in loneliness, though, and she

wanted to be face-to-face when she climaxed again, so she moved up his body to fuse her mouth with his. She tasted herself on his lips and against his tongue. Their intimacies deepened with every contact, every stroke. She felt as though she was sliding beneath the surface of a pool, and she had no desire to save herself from drowning.

"I need you, Jacinda," he whispered hotly in her ear.

She straddled him, her knees on either side of his torso, her face very close to his. The look of absolute hunger in his vivid eyes stole her breath. "Protection?" she managed to ask.

"My wallet."

She managed to lean back and snatch his jeans from the floor. Quickly finding the condom and rolling it on, she positioned herself above him, smiling at the idea of being on top.

"You liked it best this way, as I recall," he said.

"Definitely."

She lowered her hips in one smooth needy move and arched her back when he was completely inside her. The penetration was deep and sent tingles of pleasure dancing through her body. She rolled her hips to amplify the sensations and would have been content to move along at that pace for a while.

But Gideon was apparently in no mood for slow and easy.

He gripped her hips and moved her up and down, while his own hips surged upward. Intense need was chasing him, and Jacinda well knew the feeling. She braced her hands on either side of his head and met him, thrust for thrust. In seconds, her climax was on the brink, the tension in her lower belly squeezing the very breath from her body.

When the sensations within her exploded, his neck

arched, his hands clenched her sides and she knew he followed.

She reveled in the fierce pulses and gasped for air as they strengthened, then waned a little, then surged again.

She was fairly certain her pulse rate would return to normal eventually.

But she wouldn't bet on it.

JACINDA WOKE to a ringing in her ears.

Maybe it was the angels playing an anthem in her honor. Maybe it was collateral damage from the night of great sex. Maybe she'd been knocked half-unconscious by a gang of bandits hell-bent on kidnapping the cats.

No, it was just the phone.

She rolled away from the warm body next to her and stretched out her arm, knocking a picture to the floor before finally wrapping her hand around the cordless phone. Without opening her eyes, she spoke into the receiver. "It's Sunday morning at o-dark-thirty. This better be damn good."

"It certainly is, Ms. Barrett," her boss said in a snippy tone.

Jacinda's eyes popped open. She sat straight up in bed, shoving her tangled hair out of her eyes. "Mr.—Mr. Pascowitz. Sir," she added, feeling her face heat.

"There's been an incident at the auction house. I need you here right away."

"What's wrong?" Gideon asked.

Jacinda mutely shook her head at him and turned away from the sight of the lean muscles ripping across his bare shoulders and chest so she could concentrate on talking to her boss. "Incident, sir?" She swallowed hard. "What kind of incident?"

"The worst kind. A break-in. A *theft*."

Her heart pounded. A bead of sweat rolled down her back. She had to ask the question, though, somehow, part of her already knew. "What was stolen?"

"The Veros emerald."

"GET OUT OF THE CAB, Gideon."

The insane, stubborn man simply shook his head. "I'm coming with you."

She *had* to get rid of him. If she showed up at the auction house with the man who wanted the emerald, who said the emerald was already his, who just happened to be her past—and present—lover…

She shuddered. The fallout couldn't even be considered.

"You can't come. I can't be seen with you."

His head jerked back. "I want to be there for you. I *need* to be there for me. That's my—"

"You *can't* come. This is auction house business. The police won't let you in."

"I can get around—"

"No, not this time." She had to stay calm, reason with him, even though she doubted she'd ever be calm again.

How far would Gideon go to get his family's emerald back? A man who grew up with the wealth and privilege he had, as well as a man who listed "treasure hunter" on his resume, wasn't likely to take no for an answer for long. Had he done something drastic? Had he decided to circumvent the system and reacquire the stone in his own way?

Had he broken the law? Had he masterminded this theft?

What would happen when the police looked at the security tapes and saw she and Gideon had been together in the vault? What if they started digging into her past and his? Their relationship would be exposed. Along with her secrets.

She broke out in a cold sweat just thinking about it.

And, besides the impact on her job, she was having an even deeper, more personal reaction. Had their whole time together been a lie?

It was unimaginable that she could be so gullible, so taken in. Gideon was a free spirit, a live-for-the-moment guy. Surely he couldn't plan something so insidious. Surely he wouldn't betray her on such a basic level.

Still, in the days ahead, when her boss told the police about Gideon's claims on the emerald, would she have to offer herself as his alibi?

Oh, no. She couldn't. She *wouldn't*.

"How do you think it would look if I showed up with the man claiming the emerald—the recently *stolen* emerald—belongs to him?"

Gideon's eyes darkened in anger. "We have nothing to hide. We've done nothing wrong."

"Hey, lady, you want I should go?" the cabbie asked in a heavy Brooklyn accent, clearly irritated.

"No," Jacinda said.

"Yes," Gideon said at the same time.

The cabbie hit his meter. "It's gonna be a long frickin' day."

"Go," Gideon said. "We'll argue on the way."

With a brief apology in his dark eyes, the cabbie met Jacinda's gaze in the mirror, then pulled into traffic.

Men. They always stuck together.

"We can't show up together. You've made a case for the emerald. I'm in charge of selling it. Now, it's been stolen. Somebody's going to ask some pretty serious questions if we appear having just rolled out of my bed."

"Where we've been and what we've been doing is none of their business."

Jacinda rubbed her temples. Dear heaven, this wasn't a gossip rag asking questions. "It's a police investigation, Gideon. I'm pretty sure they're going to ask the whereabouts of all the people with even the slightest connection to the stone."

"It's *my* emerald. Don't you think I'm anxious to cooperate with the investigation?"

"Sure you are. On your terms. And it's not your emerald. Nothing has been proven."

"You still don't believe me," he said in a tight voice.

"It's not a question of belief," she answered, trying to stay calm.

What happened to fun? To easy and predictable? How had things gotten so out of control so quickly? Why hadn't she stuck to her vow to avoid impulsiveness like the plague?

"Damn it," she said hotly, "I don't want you with me!"

He looked almost as surprised as she felt by her outburst. "None of this looks good for either of us. You're with me on the night of the theft? What are the odds of that?"

"Pretty low, I'll admit, but—" He stopped as his gaze connected with hers. He had to see the doubt she felt. "Oh, I get it now. You think I took it."

"Clearly you didn't," she said, trying to dispel her own anxieties. "You were a little busy."

"But I could have hired somebody. I could have been, ah...*distracting* you, so the big theft could go down."

She said nothing. Hadn't she been thinking just that?

He leaned close. His lips nearly touched her ear, his body warmth spread through her, reminding her of his allure, of the pleasure and escape he offered. "Don't you think I would have been more effective if I distracted the security guard? Or maybe if I'd wined, dined and screwed the vault security systems engineer? That's a much better use of my skills, isn't it?"

The underlying sense of betrayal and insult made her stomach churn. "Gideon, I didn't mean—"

"Yes, you did." He looked away. "Stop the cab."

The cabbie pulled over, and Gideon had the door open before it even rolled to a stop. He tossed two twenties at her. "For the fare."

She watched the money float to the seat of the cab as Gideon slammed the door. Men used to toss money at her six nights a week. The action was deliberate. She'd hurt him, so he was hurting her back.

Oddly enough, she was flattered that she *could* hurt him. Not that she'd get the opportunity to find out how deeply the wounds went. Virtually accusing your lover of grand theft tended to dampen the fires of passion.

"We still goin' to Callibro's, lady?" the cabbie asked.

Unable to meet his gaze after the drama he'd witnessed, she glanced out the window. "Yes. Thank you."

They rode in silence for several blocks, and Jacinda allowed herself to briefly relive the connection and heat she'd shared with Gideon. His touch was sometimes gentle, sometimes demanding, and he always seemed to know which one she needed. He was a remarkable, intelligent, sensitive man. Their chemistry was fantastic.

Why had she thrown that away on unfounded suspicions?

"Something goin' on at the end of the block?" the cabbie asked, bringing her thoughts back to the professional crisis she was facing. "Can't get any closer."

Jacinda leaned forward to look out the front window and noticed flashing lights atop several police cars that were parked crookedly against the curb in front of the auction house.

It was real. The building's elaborate, seemingly unbreakable security system had been compromised. The emerald was gone.

"I'll get out here," she said quietly to the cabbie.

She stepped out of the car half a block from the brick-fronted building. She always looked forward to coming to work each day, to facing a new challenge and basking in past accomplishments.

Today, in the early dawn of Sunday, the city noise at a minimum, she paused on the sidewalk and blinked back unexpected tears.

Two police officers guarded the front doors. Barricades blocked the area at the front of the building.

Police. Barricades.

It was unimaginable. Like TV news clips she watched every day and never dreamed she'd see for real. She wanted to dismiss the sight.

Growing up, the apartment complex where she'd lived had been the scene of some incident or other twice a week. But not here. Crime and suffering, poverty and violence, weren't supposed to follow her to this elegant, privileged place.

Callibro's security was so thorough. How could someone have even gotten in the building undetected, much less gotten in the warehouse and vault to steal a valuable gem? She refused to think of Gideon, of the behind-the-scenes peek she'd given him. There had to be a logical explanation for why that particular emerald was taken.

Wait a second.

Surely more than just the emerald was missing. That was the only piece Mr. Pascowitz had mentioned, but more items had to have been stolen. No thief would go to the extreme trouble of getting into the building and the vault, only to walk away with one gem.

Feeling slightly more assured, she started toward the barricades. She needed to find Mr. Pascowitz and discuss their next step.

At least there were no curiosity seekers. They would come, along with the reporters, their cameras taping, their microphones extended for interviews. For now, however, they had a reprieve. While the robbery wasn't as big as an explosion impacting hundreds of people, it was newsworthy.

"You press?" the cop posted at the barricade asked, glancing behind her as if expecting a camera crew.

"No. I work at the auction house. Jacinda Barrett." She held up her employee credentials. "I believe Mr. Pascowitz is expecting me."

The officer moved aside the barrier, then escorted her to the entrance.

"Do you know what happened?" she asked as they walked.

"Call came in at three-twenty from the security system. We got here three minutes later. You want more, you gotta talk to the lieutenant. He's inside." Her escort nodded to the officer standing guard. "She's all right, Howie."

"Thanks—" Jacinda glanced at her escort's brass name tag "—Officer Santoni. It's pretty early to be working."

Santoni shrugged. "Hey, that's the breaks on the night shift." He grinned briefly before he turned to walk away. "At least it wasn't a jumper."

Jacinda headed toward Mr. Pascowitz's office, wondering if he'd called in the rest of the staff as well, or if he'd chosen her alone since the auction was her responsibility.

Regardless, she was about to become a focal point of the investigation. Her boss was bound to tell the police about Gideon's ownership claims. How long could she possibly expect to avoid questions about her connection to him?

How long before the police wanted to know where she was during the theft? How long before she was a major suspect in a multimillion-dollar robbery?

How long did she realistically have?

Hours? Minutes?

Nobody was going to listen to her, Jacinda Barrett, assistant curator, former exotic dancer, born into poverty.

"Can I help you?" a deep voice from behind her asked.

Jumping, she turned to face a man with messy, sandy-blond hair, a wrinkled baby blue shirt and navy pants. He looked as though he'd just rolled out of bed.

That seems to be going around.

"Ma'am?" he asked, walking closer.

"I—" Her voice came out like a squeak—a *guilty* squeak—so she cleared her throat. "I'm Jacinda Barrett. I work here. Mr. Pascowitz called me."

"Lieutenant Capshaw," Rumpled Man said in introduction.

Apparently she'd had only *seconds.*

His gaze roamed over her, and she was grateful she'd taken the time to put on a fresh-from-the-cleaners navy pantsuit. She might not feel confident, but she could be reasonably sure she looked it.

"You're in charge of the auction," Capshaw said.

"Yes. I am. What happened?"

"The building security system, as well as the vault, was compromised. I was headed back that way. Why don't you join me?"

Jacinda wasn't sure if that was a command or request, but she nodded. Given a choice between cops and her boss, she wasn't sure where her best chances were. She had the uneasy feeling they'd both toss her to the wolves. And she didn't see how she could avoid either. "How was the system compromised?" she asked as they headed downstairs to the warehouse and its vault.

"Slickly."

"Yet the alarm sounded."

The lieutenant raised his eyebrows.

"The officer outside told me they were called by the automated alarm." She paused, not wanting to get Santoni in trouble. "Only after I showed him my credentials, of course."

"Of course. I guess your boss's call got you out of bed."

"At four thirty in the morning that's where most people are."

"True. But were you?"

"Yes."

"Alone?"

Jacinda was beginning to think that Capshaw's rumpled appearance was a put-on. Or maybe he just didn't care about personal hygiene. Either way, she wasn't about to cower and confess to something she'd had no part in and boldly decided to be insulted by his personal question. "No, Lieutenant, I wasn't alone. Should I e-mail you a list of my current acquaintances and sexual history?"

He opened the door at the end of the hall and held it open for her. "Not yet. But stay available."

Though her heart beat at a hundred miles an hour, she nodded coolly as she passed him. "I'll need a list of the items taken as soon as possible."

"That would be a singular item, Ms. Barrett. An emerald weighing twenty-one point four karats. Are you familiar with it?"

She stopped in her tracks and stared at him. There was no hiding her surprise this time. Why would somebody break in for only one thing, even if that one thing was as lovely and valuable as that particular stone? Why not clean out the whole gem case?

Unless there was only one object of any interest. And the list of people with that much interest in this object was very, very short.

"Yes, of course," she said finally, hoping she sounded competent rather than scared. "The Veros family emerald. It's quite extraordinary."

"How much would you say a stone like that is worth?"

"It's appraised at just under two million, but with the excitement of an auction, it's possible it will sell for more."

"Is it the single most valuable gem you have in the vault?"

She swallowed. "No."

"So somebody was specifically targeting that particular stone."

"It would seem so."

"WHAT THE HELL'S GOING ON, Santoni?" Gideon barked into his cell phone.

"Hey, man, I'm just hangin' around, shootin' the breeze in the doughnut shop. How 'bout you?"

"Get real, dude. I called the station. I know you're at the Callibro's Auction House robbery."

"Burglary."

Gideon leaned against the window of a restaurant and tried to keep from grinding his teeth. "Robbery, burglary, what's the difference?"

"A big one in the law-and-order business, pal. And one you oughta know about."

"I didn't break in to that house."

"Oh, yeah, sure. They invited you *in* the front door. You just decided to go *out* the second-story window."

"Is this where I'm supposed to thank you—again—for not hauling me to the station and throwing my misguided butt in jail?"

"Nah. Forget it. I'm just messin' with you 'cause I'm bored. Give me a good mugging or liquor-store robbery over this high-society stuff any day."

"How New York of you."

"Isn't it?"

"What's missing?"

"Big green sparkly rock."

"And…"

"That's it, man. All that highfalutin stuff, and the guy takes one thing. I'd have at least shoved some of those fancy stamps in my back pocket on my way out."

"You're an efficient kind of guy, aren't you? Maybe the thief got interrupted."

"Nope. Least the lieutenant doesn't think so. The guy

was long gone when we got here, and that only took three minutes. We think he might have triggered the alarm to go off after he left. Maybe even did it by remote, like some crazy James Bond thing."

"I was in that vault. Whoever got in knew what he was doing."

"Were you now?" Santoni asked, and Gideon could all but see him smirking with interest. "Maybe we'll be gettin' you at the station after all."

"Yeah, yeah. I'm sure I'll have to talk to you guys before long."

"How deep are you in this, Gideon?" Santoni's tone changed to one of concern.

"Deep enough. Do you have any leads? Any idea how the guy got in the—?"

"Ah, I'm not sure, Mom. I'll have to call you later."

Gideon drew a deep breath. "The lieutenant there?"

"Oh, yeah. I'll grab you some eggs and milk on my way home."

"After you make your delivery to Mama, meet me at Sorba's. I'll buy you lunch."

"Sure thing."

His buddy signed off, and Gideon paced.

Neither his grand mission to get the emerald back for his family, nor his efforts to get Jacinda was going in a positive direction. Since he was undoubtedly one of the last people to see the emerald, he was bound to be questioned by the police. Jacinda likely was being questioned at this moment.

She'd been right. Their appearance together at the auction house that morning would have raised way too many eyebrows. He had always preferred bravado to apology, up-front questions to behind-the-door whispers, but he recognized bravado didn't go over well in police investigations.

And it certainly wouldn't benefit Jacinda's career.

His only comfort among the anxiety of wondering what was going on and whether or not Jacinda was suffering was that Pascowitz wouldn't expose him or his claims on the emerald. At least not yet. Pascowitz would never chance offending Sophia Graystone. Unless, of course, he'd taken the emerald himself and needed to save his own ass.

But there was no way Pascowitz had the brains or the balls to get in that vault.

So who had?

After years of tracking the gem, of enduring false leads and dead ends, the gem was gone again. Gideon had been so close.

Again.

He knew his grandmother considered his quest silly, time-consuming and futile. But of all the lost treasures he'd found, this one meant the most. It was a search, not out of generosity or curiosity, or even for the thrill of succeeding. It was a search for family pride. *His* pride. The emerald didn't belong to the Veros family; it belonged to the Graystones.

Of course if the stone had remained in his grandmother's care, she probably would have given it away to benefit a charity, so he didn't have delusions of it taking a place of pride in the Graystone family collection. No, Gideon's pursuit was motivated by the injustice done to his grandmother. The gem was hers and whoever had taken it had profited instead. That person had taken what she, no doubt, would have willingly given.

And damn it, that was plain *wrong*.

The underlying honor of his search made Jacinda's suspicions of him suck that much more.

Angry at both himself and her, he headed across the block toward the restaurant where Pete Santoni would meet him when he got off his shift.

Having her continually misjudge his character and motives was infuriating. At what point had Gideon behaved so horribly that she assumed he was a manipulative criminal? As if he had a secret ring of thieves, running around planning big heists of treasures he couldn't acquire by legitimate means.

The shadiest thing he'd ever done was pay people to give him information they probably wouldn't have otherwise divulged.

Well, that, and crawl out that second-story window.

As the city came to life around him, he walked the streets, the pavement seeming to heat with every step he took. He let the ache of Jacinda's doubt roll over him anew. The soul-deep sense of loss that she didn't believe him, or in their unique connection, was way more painful than the theft of the emerald.

Did you tell her things were different this time? his conscience whispered. *Did you bother to tell her of your growing feelings?*

No. He was too busy keeping peace, seducing and assuring her things were fun and casual. He was too busy dancing around her determination to treat him as a casual lay, an itch to scratch. He was too busy striding toward his own goals that he didn't notice how they might compromise hers.

This investigation could uncover her secret past and compromise the career she'd fought so hard for. No matter how she felt about him and his integrity, he couldn't let that happen.

No matter how much she doubted him, he believed in her.

7

"YOU'RE PREPARED to make the phone calls, aren't you, Ms. Barrett?"

Exhaustion threatened to overwhelm her, so Jacinda braced her hand against her desk. "Yes, Mr. Pascowitz," she said calmly, though there were times, like now, she wanted to grind his bow tie–wearing butt into dust. "Once the staff arrives, I'll send them to the conference room for your meeting, then I'll pull a few key people aside to call vendors and patrons."

"Make sure Andrew is one of them. His calm demeanor will be reassuring."

"Of course." Though Pascowitz had obviously never seen Mr. Calm Demeanor at a Celine Dion concert. The guy was a *fan.*

She crossed to the other side of her office to open the curtains, hoping her boss would take the hint that she was ready to tackle her workload, and he could scram anytime.

When she reached the curtains, though, something nudged her shoulder. "What the—" she said, jumping before she noticed Gideon standing behind the long yards of elegant silk. He lifted his finger to his lips.

"Ms. Barrett?" her boss said, his voice high with alarm.

Of course he didn't move toward her, and if the

Emerald Bandit had been hiding behind the curtains, she most certainly would have been taken hostage and dragged from the room by now.

"I…" She met Gideon's gaze for a moment before whirling away from the curtains. "Wow, there's so much dust." She prayed her voice didn't sound as panicked as she felt. What the devil was he doing here? How had he gotten in her office? She'd been defending him—or at least trying to talk herself out of convicting him without more proof—and he was breaking in to the very place she'd worried he'd broken in to.

Cutting off her racing thoughts, she took a deep breath. "I'll have to talk to the cleaning service about that dust right away," she said to Pascowitz. "It's probably best to leave the curtains closed. The press will be looking for any opening."

Pascowitz raised his nobby chin. "Those vultures are already circling."

"It's going to be a big story."

He sniffed derisively. "Our clients shouldn't be subjected to such indignities."

Jacinda pressed her lips together. She wanted to protect their clients, too, but the police needed cooperation to find the emerald. And the sooner they did that, the sooner Gideon would be gone and she could move on with her life.

Alone.

"Mmm, well…" She forced a smile. "I guess I should get busy reassuring all those important clients."

"Did you find Lieutenant Capshaw's questions overly taxing?"

Surprised by his show of concern, she shook her head.

"No. He mostly questioned me about our security policies and access to the vault. It's all documented electronically and manually, of course, so it seemed redundant to tell him."

Mr. Pascowitz, showing wildly uncharacteristic weariness, slid into the chair in front of her desk. "What am I supposed to tell Mr. Nash and his grandmother? The Veroses were furious. Can you imagine how he'll react?"

Her heart jumped. "Have you told the police about Mr. Nash's ownership claims?"

"No, no, that's a private matter for now. The Veros family owns it, and they hold a substantial insurance policy. If the emerald is never recovered, they will be able to collect on the policy. Hopefully, the police will recover the stone, then we can go to the board with the *delicate situation.*"

"We?" Jacinda did not, in no way, want to be involved in the ownership battle of the emerald.

"Of course. This auction, and everything in it, is *your* responsibility, is it not?"

"Yes, and I'm grateful for the opportunity."

But Pascowitz didn't seem to notice her confidence or compliment. "You know," he said as he slowly rose to his feet, "it's entirely possible I'll be called upon to soothe Mrs. Graystone over this incident."

"We can only hope."

Pascowitz shot her a questioning glare.

"She's such a valuable client."

"How right you are." His good mood restored, Pascowitz headed toward the door. "You're doing a wonderful job, Ms. Barrett. Don't worry. The show will go on, as they say on Broadway, and so we shall as well." He sailed out.

The moment the door closed, Gideon emerged from his hiding place. "Is he always that big of an ass?"

"Always." She glanced at him. "It's a little bit clichéd, ducking behind the curtains, isn't it?"

"I don't know, accusing your lover of theft was a popular plot in old movies."

She lifted her chin, though the idea of him plotting, instigating, or masterminding the theft of the emerald suddenly seemed abhorrent to her. The man who'd come to her, offering spaghetti and champagne instead of anger and judgment, couldn't possibly be responsible for something this underhanded.

Still, she had other issues with Mr. Nash. Namely, his presence in her office when she'd asked him to stay away. He was determined to control everything, to make decisions that affected her without consulting her.

"What are you doing here?" she demanded.

"Looking for you. We have a lot to talk about." He raised his eyebrows. "I'm assuming we're allowed to talk now."

Her face flamed at her directive from last night. She was determined to not let him distract her, however. "How did you get in here?"

"Officer Santoni is a friend. A friend with an excellent spaghetti sauce recipe, by the way."

His nonchalance was driving her crazy.

The man was ruining her. Her life had been clear and simple before he'd charged back into it. She'd known where she was going and why.

Now, in the span of a few days, he had her doubting her goals and ambitions. He made her body weak and clouded her mind. He jeopardized her job and the secrets of her past. He made her want him, then doubt him, then doubt her doubting him.

Choosing to focus on the theft instead of her feelings, she fisted her hands by her sides. "So I guess you know everything."

"If you mean the emerald was the only thing stolen, a seemingly unbreakable security system was breached and the police don't have a clue who did it?" He slid his arm around her waist and tugged her toward him. She tried to pretend she didn't crave his strong, reassuring touch. "Then, yeah." His eyes turned dark and smoky as his gaze roved her face. "I know everything. Even before that idiot Pascowitz laid it all out so conveniently. How do you stand him every day?"

"Yoga in the morning. Kickboxing at night."

"How...*stimulating.*"

"You're not diverting my attention to sex."

He put on a look of absolute innocence. "Is that what I was doing? I thought we were simply talking about the case."

"This is *not* your case. You need to stay as far away from here as possible. Lieutenant Capshaw is already questioning my alibi for last night. It won't take long for him to come to you."

His gaze softened as if he actually understood the panic churning in her gut. "Only because I was in the vault. You heard Pascowitz. He won't tell them about my ownership claims."

"So no one has to know about us."

He stroked her cheek, his eyes full of regret. "They will. We have to give them our alibi and get ourselves off the suspect list."

Her stomach bottomed out. "No. I can't."

"Yes, you can. And you can count the lieutenant to be fair and discreet."

"I guess you know him, too."

"Only by reputation. Like I said, Santoni is a good friend. I'll let him share the story of our first meeting sometime." He brushed her hair off her face. "You'll like it."

She liked him touching her. Way too much. But she was still wary and confused. She didn't trust him, of course, and she sensed his entrance in her life might lead her down a divergent path she'd never anticipated taking. She wasn't sure she had the courage to go down that road.

Yet no matter how many years had passed, no matter how often she told herself he was just a good time, no matter her doubts, she was still drawn to him, *connected* to him.

Maybe it was time to stop accusing and start understanding.

She met his gaze, relishing the heat she received in return. "Why didn't you force your way into the building, play the arrogant Graystone heir and tell the police and Pascowitz the emerald is yours?"

"I could say I was thinking of you. And while that's certainly true, there's another reason—self-protection. Gran's going to be ticked when she finds out that damn rock caused all this trouble."

She angled her head. *"Damn rock?"*

He cupped her cheek. "She thinks I'm an idiot for trying to find it. She could care less if it's found."

"And you never bothered to mention that because…"

"*I* want to find it, and her name opens doors."

"Why do you want to find it?"

"Pride."

She searched his gaze. There was more. "And?"

"It's the right thing to do."

Coming from anybody else, she would have smirked, but Gideon made her believe it.

His brutal honesty loosened most of the knot of tension in her stomach. The emerald meant more to him than a mere conquest. Was it possible she did, too? And how would she feel if that were true?

The realization that they both had so much at stake was scary and comfortable at the same time. One thing was for certain—they were in this together now. And together they would have to find a way to make it all right again.

"If we find the emerald before the cops, we can keep ourselves off the suspect list, plus keep your grandmother's disinterest and my past a secret."

His eyes widened. "That's supposed to be my line."

"Yeah, well, I thought I'd be the adventurous one this time. Deal?"

"Deal," he said, "but I have a question first."

"Fine. I've got one, too."

"Are we just a one-night stand?"

She studied him for a moment. "I'm not sure. Did you take that emerald?"

"No."

"Then no." His gaze dropped to her lips, and she shook her head. She was fully under his spell again, but she wasn't letting him off easy. "My life was perfect before you came back into it, you know."

"Mine was pretty comfortable, too."

"So now we're diving into hell together?"

"It would seem so."

"Fine."

She pulled his head toward her and fused their lips.

GIDEON SANK into his own little piece of heaven and decided Jacinda's lips should be bronzed.

Though that would spoil their lush softness, and that would be a crying shame.

He angled his head to take their kiss deeper, so he could sweep his tongue inside and really taste her. She was in his arms again, hungering for his touch instead of scowling at him and doubting him.

He didn't want to remember the sense of panic and betrayal he'd felt earlier in the cab, when she'd looked at him with suspicion in her eyes. Instead, he focused on their renewed connection and her admission that he wasn't a one-night stand.

There was something between them that couldn't be denied. The emotions were real. And though he had no idea how their journey would develop, he was comforted by the knowledge that they'd find out together.

His hands sliding over her butt, he backed her across the room. "Is that desk as sturdy as it looks?"

She threaded her hands through his hair. "No, and I have to work."

"So you're kicking me out?"

She moaned against his cheek. "Definitely." He pulled her tight against his erection. "Maybe."

He smiled, then trailed kisses along her jaw. "So, you can come see me after work?"

"Yeah." She pulled back. "Bring me a list of suspects."

"I guess we're not basking in the moment."

"No. And bring all those receipts you've gathered on the sales history of emerald. You never said who stole it from your grandmother in the first place. Do you know?"

Man, the woman could turn from hot and pliant to demanding fast.

"I have some suspects," he said. *Stolen again.* Hell, what were the odds? "But I don't know for sure. I started tracking it after it was hocked."

"I think it's time to find out for sure."

"You think the same person stole it again?"

"Or maybe somebody who knows him or her. Maybe the thief couldn't stand to see it sold. Maybe he has some kind of emotional attachment."

"He sold it in a high-end pawnshop a couple of months after it was stolen, so he couldn't have been too attached."

She angled her head. "Pawnshop? Wouldn't the police have found it pretty easily there?"

"They might have—if they'd been looking for it." He winced at her confused expression. If they were going to get to the bottom of this mess, he was going to have to come clean about a lot more than just their relationship. "Gran never reported the theft to the police."

"She *what?*"

"She apparently considered it gone and didn't want to discuss it."

"*Didn't want to discuss it?* That's absurd."

"Hey, you can tell her that anytime you're feeling brave."

"It was worth a lot of money even then. She can let hundreds of thousands of dollars go—" she snapped her fingers "—like that?"

"No. She made a claim with the insurance company, telling them it was missing, so they gave her the lost item's replacement value."

"But she could have gotten full value if she'd told them that it was stolen."

"Yes, but that would have required a police report, which she didn't want to file."

"Rich people are weird."

"A lot of the time," he agreed.

"Why didn't anybody in the family try to talk sense into her?"

"Neither my mother nor I were born yet, and we seem to be the only people on the planet who ever question her about anything."

"Do you think she knows who took it?"

He sighed, having thought the same thing many times. "Seems likely, doesn't it? It would explain her lack of interest in finding it."

"And her lack of interest in you finding it now."

"You think so?" He'd wondered about that himself briefly. Gran always passed off his quest as a waste of time, but he'd begun to think lately there was more to her criticism. "After all this time? That would mean he's still alive. A lot of her friends aren't."

"If the thief was a friend, or one of her contemporaries, maybe she didn't want to embarrass him. Today, she still might not want to embarrass his descendants."

"For two million bucks, he had to have been a pretty good friend."

"Maybe he was more than a friend."

"This happened before she was married. Women of that era didn't exactly play the field."

Jacinda shrugged. "Women she knew did, and a woman would do a lot more to protect a lover than a friend."

He grabbed her hand and tugged her into his arms again. "She would, huh?"

"I don't know how you ever find anything. You can't stay focused for more than five minutes."

He kissed her jaw. "You're an unusual distraction."

"You need to— I can't think when you do that."

"Don't think. Just feel." He placed lingering kisses by her ear, flicking his tongue across the lobe. He smiled inwardly when her breathing hitched, and her pulse pounded fiercely against his lips.

"You need to talk to your grandmother," she said weakly.

"I'm having dinner at her house tonight. You could come and grill her."

"No thanks."

He leaned back. "You don't want to meet her?"

"Sure, I do—at a charity event, during an auction, in my office. She can pick any of those times and places. But I'd rather not be presented as the former exotic dancer and present lover of her grandson."

"Hey, I'm her *favorite* grandson." He tipped her chin up with his finger. "And she doesn't know anything about your past. She'd admire you, not judge you, anyway."

Her eyes reflected her continued doubts. "I don't belong in her mansion in the Hamptons."

How could a woman with such intelligence and confidence be such an idiot sometimes? She'd accomplished so much in her life already, and would no doubt continue to dazzle anybody around her. When would she stop caring so much about how she *started* her life? Nobody else did.

But he knew anger wasn't the way to break through this

barrier. "Well, then you'll be pleased to learn that she's in the city at the moment, so we're having dinner at her apartment."

"On Park Avenue."

"Naturally, but your address isn't exactly embarrassing, either. You certainly belong—"

"It's not really mine."

Argh. She was killing him. "Think of it as a field trip to appraise antiques," he said smoothly. "Surely you've done that while working here."

"Yeah, but—"

"Think of the business contacts you could make through her. So many lovely, expensive family heirlooms and pieces of history, all longing to be sold. By you."

She narrowed her eyes. "You enjoy tempting me, don't you?"

"My mission in life. Come on. It's Sunday dinner at Gran's house. How bad can it be?"

Clearly, she thought it had the potential to be disastrous, but she simply nodded. "Okay. I'll go."

"Great." He gave her a quick kiss, then backed toward her office door. "She makes everybody dress up for dinner, so you look perfect like you are. Oh, and you get a lunch break, right?"

"Probably not today."

"Well, tell Pascowitz you have a lunch date with a big-moneyed VIP."

"What big-moneyed VIP would that be?"

Pausing in the doorway, he grinned. "Me."

"WE'RE OFF THE suspect list," Gideon said, cutting in to his manicotti and marinara.

Even though it smelled delicious, Jacinda stared blankly at her grilled chicken pasta with pesto. She'd spent the morning delivering the news to clients, which hadn't been accepted gracefully by too many, and calming down other clients who'd already heard about the theft and wanted to know what kind of cracker-box operation they were running.

The whole thing was so humiliating, and she was sure her auction was irreparably tainted before it had even begun. So far, only two clients had pulled their items from the sales docket, and Jacinda knew she'd scramble the rest of the day to make sure more didn't follow.

Gideon's news about them no longer being suspects was great, even if she still doubted that her past would remain hidden.

"That was fast," she said, pushing a piece of grilled chicken around on her plate.

"Nothing's official, of course," Gideon said. "I told Santoni we were together all night, and he promised to tell his lieutenant."

"Don't you think they're going to investigate employees? When they do, my past—"

He laid his hand over hers. "Won't matter."

"But—"

"Is it likely Lieutenant Capshaw will find out you were once an exotic dancer even though I'm assuming you left it off your curator resume?"

She nodded. It was debatable that her former boss at the dance club would maintain the story that she'd been a waitress, not a dancer, under police questioning.

"You can't change the past," Gideon said quietly, "and I told you before, Capshaw won't care." He nodded at her plate. "Please eat."

Eating a bite of pesto-covered bow-tie pasta, Jacinda instantly forgot the irate clients, worried board of directors, overwrought boss and relentless press.

She dug in to her lunch with relish.

"Apparently the police have moved away from suspecting employees," Gideon said. "Getting past the security and into the vault was way too sophisticated for your average burglar.

"In the colorful words of Pete Santoni, *it was like some weird James Bond dude came through.* They found no fingerprints, no hairs or fibers, no physical evidence at all. The system outside was jammed by who-the-hell-knows-what. As I'm sure you know, the doors to restricted areas were accessed by the bar code on the bottom of an employee's credential." He nodded at the one hanging around her neck. "The ID used to get through all the doors turned out to be an employee's, but it belongs to a guy who's on vacation."

Jacinda nearly choked. "Edward Klein?"

"That's him. But he's definitely in San Francisco, and he has his ID with him. The thief had to have made a duplicate."

"But that won't get you in the gem vault, and the code changes weekly."

"Which is why the police think the thief compromised the computer system. He probably picked an employee at random."

"It can't look good, though, that we were in the vault on Thursday."

"I wasn't the only person you showed the emerald to, remember? With Santoni vouching for us, we'll be fine."

Jacinda sipped her water. "But he doesn't know me. He's vouching for me because of you."

Gideon shrugged. "Sure."

She'd never had anyone in her life who protected her without question. His effort to do so was as surprising as it was comforting.

Don't get used to it, Jacy. You don't have anybody to rely on but yourself.

Her conscience, in the form of her mother's voice, brought her back to reality with a jarring slam. She could appreciate Gideon, his caring and influence, but she wouldn't count on it.

She slid her hand over his, and he glanced up at her, his expression surprised. "Thanks."

He squeezed her fingers. "We're in this together, right, partner?"

In what? Their intimate relationship? Their business arrangement? How deep did this go? How closely entwined would their lives become?

"Yeah, I guess we are," she said finally.

They continued to discuss details and theories about the emerald's original theft and the one they found themselves in the middle of, until her boss called her cell phone and demanded she return to work.

Gideon had the restaurant hostess call a cab, then walked outside with her. "I'll pick you up at your office at six," he said.

"Do we have time for me to go home and change?"

"You look beautiful the way you are."

"I'd rather be wearing Chanel." When he looked blank, she added, "It's a girl thing."

"Okay, fine. Can I watch you change?"

She waggled her finger as the cab pulled alongside the curb. "No way. Then we'll never be on time."

"If I'm on time, my mother will faint."

"*I'll* be on time, so you will, too."

He opened the cab door and helped her inside, then leaned close. He had an oddly pleased expression on his face. "You trusted me to give Santoni our alibis."

"I had a choice?" she asked with light sarcasm.

He laid his finger over her lips. "We're bonding."

"That's probably not a good thing," she mumbled.

"Pessimist."

"Optimist."

Grinning, he kissed her once more, then closed the door.

As the cab pulled away, Jacinda felt amazingly light and cheerful. The pressure in her chest had eased, and she thought there might actually be a way out of this mess that wouldn't ruin her life. She didn't recognize the feelings coursing through her at first, then she realized she was happy. Gideon made her happy.

Well, when he wasn't making her crazy.

8

EVEN AFTER ALL Jacinda had seen and done since leaving that dirty housing complex in Las Vegas, nothing had prepared her for Sophia Graystone's luxury penthouse apartment.

The butler who opened the door was like a character from an old movie. He wore a precisely tailored and pressed black tuxedo and white gloves, and his hair was glossy silver and brushed back from his serene face as if carved from metal. He was a little scary and off-putting, but she tried to remind herself she was an invited guest.

She wondered briefly if the UPS man got the chills when he dropped off a package.

Turning away from the man, she directed her attention to the magnificent, high-ceilinged foyer. A dazzling crystal chandelier dangled above her, shooting shards of light dancing on the deeply stained wooden floor. Pale peach silk wallpaper surrounded her. Figurines posed in silent elegance on antique tables and priceless Impressionist paintings hung on the walls.

Each detail, statue and color was planned, precisely placed and artfully lighted. It was like being in a museum, only somehow warmer. The collection of objets d'art seemed loved and appreciated. No doubt dusted daily by people like the butler and his staff, but still cared for.

She shifted her gaze back to the butler, whose smooth, dignified manner didn't falter, even when Gideon greeted him with, "What's up, McElvy?"

"The moon and the stars, I believe, sir," McElvy said in a deep, perfectly modulated voice.

Nice. Maybe the butler wasn't as stiff as he seemed.

"Madame is receiving in the library," McElvy said. "As you are the first to arrive, you can join her there." He walked ahead of them down the hall, passing a room that in an old-fashioned world would have been called the parlor, with its delicate settees, soft, feminine colors and silver tea set resting on a dainty table. "And to what can we attribute your promptness, Master Gideon? Your lovely companion, perhaps?"

Master Gideon? Jacinda had to stifle a giggle, and now she was sure there was more going on beneath McElvy's stiff suit than first appeared.

"And what a shame I've yet to be introduced," McElvy continued dryly.

Gideon clutched his heart. "Did I leave my manners on the subway?"

"*Surely,* sir, you did *not* take the subway."

In answer, Gideon grinned, then he formally wrapped his hand around Jacinda's and held it out for McElvy's appraisal. "McElvy, my good man, this is Jacinda Barrett, assistant curator of Callibro's Auction House, a lady of impeccable and refined taste, and a close, personal associate of yours truly."

Feeling her face flush, Jacinda shook McElvy's hand. "He tends to go overboard sometimes."

McElvy might have smiled, but if he did, it was fleeting. "Yes, miss, he certainly does."

She angled her head. "Mrs. Graystone's home is beautiful."

"She'll be pleased to hear it."

"But I bet you're the one who keeps everything running smoothly."

McElvy certainly smiled this time, and Jacinda knew she'd hit a home run. It wasn't much different than visiting a potential client's home. Everybody liked to be appreciated for the areas where they excelled or the things they cared about. It was simply a manner of finding out what those things were.

"Would you like some champagne?" McElvy said as they approached the door of the library.

A woman standing in the corner of the room turned. She wore a vivid red pantsuit, dangling diamond earrings and her silver hair arranged around a striking and lean face. She raised her eyebrows, two dark arches above deep green eyes that matched Gideon's. "Who, exactly, are you giving away my good champagne to, McElvy?"

"Perhaps, I overstepped—"

"Gideon." The woman smiled broadly, an impish light flooding her eyes that matched one Jacinda had seen many times in her grandson. "You're early."

"Just on time for once, Gran."

Despite her welcoming smile and tone, Sophia Graystone hadn't moved. It was her house, her world to rule, after all, so Gideon grasped Jacinda's hand, and they walked down the few steps into the room, crossing the soft-looking wool carpet toward his grandmother.

Sophia's gaze shifted to Jacinda and became measuring. "And who have you brought?"

There was no doubt in Jacinda's mind that Gideon had

called his grandmother and told her precisely who he was bringing. Maybe even why. Jacinda knew she was being closely, if politely, evaluated for the next several minutes, and probably the entire night.

Is this woman here to use my grandson, his money and his name? Is she after the excitement of his treasure hunts? Is she simply dazzled by his charm and good looks?

She could all but hear the thoughts flooding Sophia's mind and couldn't help but admire them. Too bad Jacinda had no idea how she felt about Gideon, or what, exactly, she wanted from him.

"This is Jacinda," Gideon said as they reached his grandmother. "She's an old friend I've recently found again in the city."

"Jacinda." Sophia Graystone grasped her hand firmly, then released it, though her gaze never moved. "I'm so pleased to meet you. Have some champagne. I won't let McElvy call me a cheapskate."

"Thanks, but I'm f—"

"You'll have champagne," Sophia said, sliding her fingers along Jacinda's forearm.

The gesture was oddly maternal and made a lump rise in Jacinda's throat, which only served to remind her how long a day it had been and how close to the surface her emotions had risen.

With the cork popping, it seemed the choice was made, and during the pouring, toasting and settling into chairs, Jacinda had a few seconds to gather her thoughts.

"Gideon doesn't bring his girls here too often," Sophia said, sitting in a burgundy club chair opposite the love seat Jacinda and Gideon had settled into.

Gideon paused with his champagne glass against his lips. "Gran, you make it sound like I have a damn harem."

Sophia grinned, again in that mischievous way Gideon often did. "Don't let your mother hear you curse, baby. She's on a mission this week."

Gideon rolled his eyes and gulped his champagne. "What now?"

"I believe it's the Baptist Women's Missions."

"Hell."

Jacinda sipped champagne and watched her lover and his grandmother. She recognized what a rare glimpse into Gideon's life this was. How a man interacted with his family, and the respect—or lack thereof—he showed was an interesting glimpse into his character. No matter the economic level, she'd seen many dysfunctional families—and just as many who loved each other and hung in there amid the challenges, sorrows and joys.

"Naturally," Sophia said, "they want a check from me, as well. However, I'm withholding my payment for a while. Those catty women looked down on me years ago when I opened a nightclub for struggling jazz musicians as if I'd given manna to Satan himself."

"Which you'd never do," Gideon said.

Sophia leaned back in her chair. "Not unless he was dying of thirst."

For the first time since Gideon told her he wanted to take her to dinner at his grandmother's, Jacinda relaxed. Everything she'd read about Sophia Graystone was true. She was filthy rich, dignified and cultured—to a point. Beyond that, she was sassy and funny. She was also her own woman—a philanthropic institution, supportive of controversial causes without care to what anybody thought about the choices she made.

"She'll give the money eventually," Gideon said, sending his grandmother an affectionate look of admiration.

"Sure I will." Sophia's gaze locked on Jacinda's. "Everybody deserves a second chance."

She knows.

How had Jacinda really expected to come to the house of a world-renowned society queen and not be put under the microscope? Had she really thought she'd get to date/sleep with/be seen with Gideon and not have consequences? Had she really anticipated hanging out with him for the duration of the auction and not get into the rest of their lives?

The theft of the emerald had sent their relationship into warp speed and made everything so much more complicated and *real.* It all would have been so much simpler if he'd really been the penniless adventurer she'd assumed he was when they met six years ago in Vegas. One she could sleep with then abandon.

Then she wouldn't have had to examine her emotions, to worry about his feelings and hers and how they intertwined. She could have kept her wild nights in a neat column separate from her dignified days.

"Oh, Gideon, thank God you're safe."

Jacinda glanced at the doorway to see who'd spoken.

A couple appeared at the entrance to the library. The woman was delicately thin, wore a frothy pink dress and had highlighted brown hair. The man wore a dark blue suit and stood with military precision.

The woman rushed toward Gideon and sat beside him, yanking him against her chest. "I heard you were questioned by the police."

"Gran..." Gideon said, shooting an annoyed glance at his grandmother.

Sophia said nothing, looked amused and sipped from her champagne glass.

"Are you all right?" The woman, who had to be Gideon's mother, since she had the same Graystone eyes, leaned back to look at her son. "I was so afraid we'd need to bail you out."

"Again," Sophia added, looking wildly pleased.

"I'm fine, Mother," Gideon said, his face flushing. "And I wasn't *questioned* by the police. I just talked to a friend of mine who's a policeman. Gran exaggerated. Again," he added with a smirk in his grandmother's direction. "Besides, the cops rarely push hot bamboo under your fingernails these days."

His mother didn't look comforted. "The places you've been, I wouldn't be surprised."

"She's been like that all day," the military man said, walking into the room. "McElvy, I'm going to need a double scotch."

Seemingly out of the woodwork, McElvy appeared with the drink, already prepared, obviously anticipating Gideon's father's arrival. "Right here, Colonel."

"Good man." He accepted the drink, sipped, then nodded at the butler. "Excellent as always."

Jacinda stood as the man approached the love seat where she and Gideon were sitting. Since everyone else did the same, she had a moment to appreciate her training and instincts over the last few years.

This man was important.

The bearing in his shoulders, the confidence in his gaze and the smooth way he moved all swirled together to create an aura that Jacinda recognized in slightly different ways in his son.

She hadn't expected to meet Gideon's parents. He'd conveniently left that bit of info out of the dinner invitation. But if she had, would she have anticipated a pink-clad, hovering mother and formal, military father?

Ah, no.

And there was nothing like meeting the entire, über-rich society clan of your temporary lover over the subject of a multimillion-dollar emerald they'd once owned.

Gideon clutched her hand, giving it a quick squeeze.

"Jacinda, meet my parents."

GIDEON WAITED UNTIL dessert before bringing up the emerald. He'd said nothing to Gran beyond the fact that he was involved in another hot case, which was naturally the reason she'd been so gleeful earlier. At times, it seemed she lived through him and his adventures, reminding him how alike they were. Someday, he hoped to hear the tales of his own grandson's life and remind himself about the good old days, too.

Unless, God forbid, his grandson became a financial consultant or something equally boring.

But now he'd have to burst Gran's bubble of excitement. It was time she learned what his big case was and accept her role in finding a solution. He needed her cooperation, and for that, it was wise to catch her off guard.

Plus, he was positive she knew way more than she'd said about her "missing" emerald.

"So the break-in at Callibro's Auction House…" He posed the statement to the table in general, though he kept his gaze on his grandmother, who sat regally at one end.

Gran raised her eyebrows, but said nothing, and Gideon couldn't read anything into that reaction. Which was no doubt her intent.

"How awful," his mother said, her eyes widening. "Jacinda, isn't that where Gideon said you work? You poor thing, having to do your job under those conditions. I hope they're seeing to your safety. We should all say a special prayer tonight."

"Thank you for your concern," Jacinda said, seeming surprised by the outpouring of attention. "It's fine, really."

His mother offered Gideon her brightest smile. "Is that why you invited Jacinda to dinner? That's my sweet boy. Charity begins at home."

Jacinda's face paled at the word *charity,* and Gideon laid his arm across the back of her chair, giving her shoulder a light squeeze.

"I sincerely doubt Jacinda needs our charity, Betsy," his father said.

His mother sniffed importantly. "Well, she certainly needs our prayers. I'm chairing a fund-raising campaign for the Baptist Women's Missions, Jacinda. I'll be sure to put your name on our list."

"That's very gracious. Thank you."

Smooth, Gideon reflected. The woman was smooth as silk. And not just her skin.

She had to be slightly embarrassed that an unknown group of Baptist women would now think her life was a mess, even if she could appreciate the sentiment.

But he had to admit his mother's effervescence was a welcome intrusion into the tension and chaos that had been layered over the entire day.

"Don't you use Callibro's, Sophia?" his father asked.

"Yes, I do," Gran said, her gaze flicking to Jacinda, to whom she offered a faint smile. "They're a fine establishment. Malle would be proud."

"Jacinda says they're holding up okay," Gideon said, not about to let his grandmother distract him from his goal. "It helps that the police are leaning toward somebody from the outside, but it has to be unnerving to work around cops fingerprinting everyone and dusting everything for prints."

Jacinda nudged his knee with hers under the table.

He probably should have shared his strategy to try to guilt his grandmother into helping, but he was used to working alone, so he hadn't thought of it. Besides, Jacinda would catch on quick enough.

"They fingerprinted you?" his mother asked, horrified.

"Yes, but it wasn't a big deal. I'm in the vault all the time. It would be odd if my fingerprints *weren't* there." Jacinda shot Gideon an annoyed glare. "And everything's going fine at the office. We're moving forward as scheduled with the auction on Wednesday, so it's a matter of adjusting some of the final details."

"Let me know if you have any problems," his father said, his tone commanding but kind. "I think you'll be able to count on the police to be discreet, though. Malle was an important woman in the city and always supported law enforcement. It's the insurance agents that will make your life a living hell."

"Thurston!" his mother said, setting down her coffee cup with a clang.

"Good grief, Betsy. God knows there's a hell." His attention slid to Jacinda again. "How big was your loss?"

"That's the odd thing, Father," Gideon said before

Jacinda could again downplay the theft, which, he had to admit, wasn't normal polite dinner conversation. "Only one item was taken."

"One?" His father's eyebrows moved together. "Who would go to the trouble to break in to a fortress like the auction house, then steal *one* thing?"

Gideon's gaze flicked to Gran. "We certainly would all like to know the answer to that question."

Typically, his grandmother gave no reaction at all. She didn't even blink.

Gideon had often thought he'd inherited his considerable skill at poker—which had come in handy on more than one case—from her.

"What did they take?" his mother asked.

"An emerald," Gideon said. "A large one. Twenty-one point four karats."

Gran sipped her coffee, which was telling in itself. The resemblance to her emerald didn't get past her. *Nothing* got past her.

And normally Gran asked him all kinds of details about his cases. The fact that she looked bored as a turnip was significant.

"It's owned by the Veros family," Jacinda said, her hand brushing his side. "Do you know them, Mrs. Graystone?"

Ah, the clever Jacinda catches on. Maybe teamwork would come naturally to him after all.

"They were quite upset when my boss called them earlier," Jacinda said. "I think it's possible they'll sue."

"No, I don't know anyone by that name offhand," Gran said. "I could check with my secretary when she arrives in the morning."

Jacinda smiled politely. "That would be wonderful.

The auction house takes security very seriously. No one can figure out how the thief got in."

Though she couldn't possibly know, the subject of security tickled his father's interest.

"When I was in the military, I dealt in security issues," he said. "Perhaps I can offer some insight." He shot Gideon an affectionately annoyed glance. "My son never lets me in on his cases. Too much pride to ask the old man for help."

"I'd be glad to hear your suggestions," he said to his father.

Jacinda sent him what she probably meant to be a mildly affectionate look, but it turned him on. They'd gone from intimate, to suspicion and doubt, to cautious cooperation, then partners in the past seventeen hours. When they were alone again, they had some lingering issues to settle.

And he wanted to solve them all naked and horizontal.

Though he wouldn't say no to vertical—the wall or the shower stall would do.

"They told me next to nothing about the break-in," she said, turning toward his father, "but Gideon got some information from his friend, I think."

"They're leaning toward somebody from the outside," Gideon said. "So far, the employees check out, and the ID the thief used to get into the warehouse belonged to an employee who's on vacation. The thief also knew the vault code."

"So the computer security was compromised," his father said, wrinkling his forehead. When Gideon nodded, he turned toward Jacinda. "You have an overall security system as well as a separate one for the vault, I assume."

"Yes."

"And night guards," his father said.

"The guard was knocked unconscious," Gideon said. "The police think it was some kind of gas forced through the air-conditioning ducts. Then the thief crawled out of the vents, shut down the security system from the guard's computer station, made his way to the vault and used the employee's ID and code to get through all the necessary doors."

"Very neat and professional," his father commented.

"Professional seems right."

His mother angled her head. "Do you mean someone hired a thief?" A half smile formed on her lips. "It was probably somebody from the Chinese government. I saw this movie last week where this group of ninjas were going to steal back all the Chinese jade throughout the world—"

His father patted his mother's hand. "Betsy, please. Let Gideon finish."

"Hiring someone with that much expertise would be very expensive. Do you agree, sir?" he asked his father.

"I do. I suspect whoever hired the thief would also have to pay or otherwise convince him to take only the emerald. It would be very risky to enter into that kind of agreement with a criminal."

Jacinda leaned back in her chair. "So we're dealing with a smart, experienced thief, and a rich, clever employer."

Gideon glanced down the table at Gran, who was watching them all silently, a faint smile on her lips. She fit the employer's description to a *T*.

And while that might have seemed a bizarre thought to

have about one's grandmother, Gideon wouldn't count out anything when thinking about his.

Still, why would she take an emerald she wanted nothing to do with? After Wednesday, the stone would have been transferred to a new owner, maybe even an anonymous one, and possibly lost to them forever.

But then he hadn't intended to let that happen.

"This is all too disturbing," his mother said, rising from the table. "I'll get the cards, and we can play bridge."

Gideon rose, then pulled out Jacinda's chair. "We can't, Mother. We still need to go through my research tonight. I've got to give all the information I can to the police."

As Jacinda turned toward him, she raised her eyebrows briefly, knowing very well he wasn't going to do that.

Everyone else, though, seemed to accept his excuse and wished them a good evening.

Well, *almost* everyone else.

"I'd like a moment alone with my grandson," Gran said as she stood. Suddenly, she was no longer smiling.

"JUST WHAT ARE YOU UP TO, Gideon Michael Nash?" Gran asked the moment the library door was closed.

"I'm getting back your emerald." He flopped on the sofa. "I thought you'd be appreciative."

"I told you to let it go," she said, standing in front of him and glaring.

"You knew I wouldn't, though," he said in a cheerful tone, pretending he didn't notice her anger. "And I almost had it, too. But then somebody stole it. You got any idea what that's about?"

"Of course not."

He lowered his eyelids to slits, but still watched her

closely. The frustration she'd hidden so carefully earlier had risen to the surface. "But you know something about the emerald that you haven't told me."

"That emerald is not mine."

"Yes, it is."

"You don't have any proof."

"But I do." He rose slowly and pulled a small stack of pictures from his coat pocket. That minicamera his father had given him had come in handy again. He'd have to remind the "old man" that he'd helped Gideon solve his cases many times over. Jacinda would be pissed he'd taken shots of the gem in the vault, but Gideon had learned long ago that showing your hand during the first round of betting was never a wise move.

He handed his grandmother the pictures and watched her thumb through them.

After a couple of moments, she handed them back and glanced up at him, her face void of expression. "This stone is certainly similar to the one I used to own. But there have to be dozens, hundreds like it."

She knew the unusual color and size made her statement beyond likely. Hadn't one of her own friends relished describing it to Gideon nearly a dozen years ago, lighting his fascination with the stone in the first place? "Don't you want to see him pay—whoever took the necklace from you?"

"Oh, Gideon, please." She turned away. "It's been sixty years. Who cares anymore?"

"I do. Somebody took advantage of you, and I won't let them get away with it."

She stiffened and glanced at him over her shoulder. "What makes you think somebody took advantage of me?"

"I know you. You probably left the necklace carelessly lying on the bedside table. You trust people. You believe in their character, and I won't let anybody get away with betraying that trust."

She abruptly laid her palm against his cheek. "You're such a good grandson."

Surprised to feel a lump of emotion rise in his throat, he grasped her hand and kissed her palm. "You're okay, too. For an old granny."

"Pah. Keep that up, boy, and I'll cut you out of my will."

"You don't need one. You're gonna live forever." He squeezed her hand. When he spoke, he'd dropped all the teasing from his voice, but was still careful to keep his tone soft. "What happened to the emerald, Gran?"

"I hear one was stolen yester—"

"Don't." He shook his head. "You know this Veros one and yours are the same. What happened?"

Sighing, she released his hand and stepped back. "Let me look at my diaries and remember fully. We'll talk tomorrow."

"And you'll tell me what you know?"

"I'll tell you what I can," she said firmly, and Gideon knew no amount of prodding would get him any more information. "You go see to your beautiful lady."

Knowing he'd been dismissed, Gideon headed toward the door, but he paused when his grandmother spoke again. "In fact, maybe if you tell me more about her, I'll tell you more about that stone."

Since he had no idea how he felt about what was going on between him and Jacinda—or how he planned to resolve his evolving feelings—he shook his head. "You're a clever woman, Gran."

She blew him a kiss. "And don't you forget it."

9

As THE CAB PULLED AWAY from the curb, Gideon gripped the back of Jacinda's neck and kissed her long and deep.

"What was that for?" she asked when they parted, her head spinning and her lips tingling.

"You're amazing. *We're* amazing. What a team. Jab, retreat, jab, jump to the side. It was beautiful."

Having no idea what he was talking about, Jacinda stared at him. "You have completely lost your mind."

"Wouldn't be the first time," he said with a shrug. "And I don't have a harem."

"O-kay."

"I'm crazy about you," he said in a rush before he pressed his lips to hers again.

Though still wildly confused, Jacinda gave herself over to the moment. The nervous tension that had consumed her while she stood outside the library door melted away in an instant. Gideon's warmth and familiar taste swamped her with desire. She laid her hands on his chest, delighting in the feel of his heart racing beneath her fingertips.

He was amazing, and they were definitely amazing together.

She guessed the jabbing and retreating he'd been babbling about involved their teamwork questioning at dinner. They'd picked up on each other's cues and threw his family off balance, though she wondered how much they'd actually accomplished with his grandmother.

Still, the whole thing had been wildly exciting, which she hadn't expected. She could certainly see the allure of this treasure-hunting business Gideon loved so much.

Could they be into each other even deeper than they were in this jewel heist case?

Their journey from intimacy, through doubt to partnership had been a fast and furious one that showed no signs of slowing down. And while there was a level of trust within her that he probably would never achieve, no one would, she'd let him closer to her heart than anybody.

"What did you find out from your grandmother?" she asked against his lips, hoping to remind him that they were in a cab, and this making out couldn't go too far. As in the restaurant on Thursday night, they tended to forget their surroundings when they touched.

"Not much." His hand snaked under her jacket and blouse, sliding up beneath her bra to her breast. "We're talking tomorrow."

"Tomorrow? Why then?"

"She wants to look over her diaries."

Sounded like stalling to her. "Is the emerald hers?"

His thumb flicked across her nipple. "You're doubting me?"

Her stomach clenched, and she gasped. "Oh, ah…no." The man was *incredible* with his hands. "Did she *admit* the emerald was hers?"

"Pretty much."

She leaned back. "*Pretty much.* That's it? What's happening? What does she know?"

"She knows plenty," he said against her neck, his lips tracing a burning line up to her ear.

His lips were also incredible, and as Jacinda's thighs started to tingle, she figured this whole conversation was better saved for another time.

She slid her hand down the front of his crisply pressed white shirt. "I've never seen you in a suit."

He pushed up the hem of her skirt, and he found the needy heat between her legs quickly. "Hate 'em."

Leaning back in the corner of the seat, his body blocking her view of the driver in the front—and, hopefully, his view of her—she looked her lover over. "I like it. Sexy." She trailed her fingers through the long, silky locks of his hair. "I could do without the tie, though."

He pushed aside her panties, his fingers sliding up inside her. "Could you?"

Her breathing stopped, then started again in a violent rush as his thumb found her clitoris, and his fingers moved rhythmically in and out of her body. Leave it to Gideon to push the boundaries of making out in public. Again.

Feeling like a guppy flopping on the sand, she somehow made her hands work long enough to loosen his tie and unbutton the top button on his shirt. Then she simply gave herself over to the intense pleasure only Gideon seemed capable of bringing her.

Her whole body tightened, anticipating the next stroke, the next wet kiss on her neck, the next puff of hot breath. She knew she could come at any second. She knew only he could make it happen. She clung to him, gripping his shoulders, closing her eyes against sensual weakness, while at the same time reveling in her surrender.

After the day she'd had, she deserved a damn orgasm.

And by arching her back, and Gideon moving his thumb just the right way, at just the right moment and speed, she got one.

It was intense and long, her hips bucking with every pulse, her heart jumping in time.

She was pretty sure she moaned. She didn't think she screamed, but either way, she didn't care.

It wasn't the first wild thing to happen in an NYC cab, and she doubted it would be the last.

When the pulses faded, she cupped Gideon's cheek. "I needed that."

Smiling, he kissed her lightly. "I figured you did."

When the cab stopped a couple of minutes later, she glanced out the window, not realizing until she saw her apartment building where they were.

Gideon helped her out, then, as he paid the cabbie, she heard the driver say, "Hey, man, anytime."

She and Gideon had probably given their cab drivers enough fantasy material for the next month.

They linked hands on the sidewalk, and Jacinda forced herself to transform briefly into the respectable executive she was by nodding politely to the doorman. But after they entered the elevator, her mind turned completely to Gideon, the pleasure he'd given her, the pleasure she wanted to give him and the whole, long night ahead.

Her self-imposed drought had undoubtedly made her more sensitive, made her need the release even more. It couldn't be *him,* could it? It couldn't be this connection, this unique chemistry they shared.

Anybody would have picked up on the questioning of his family. Though he seemed subtle, anybody who knew about the case, and knew Gideon, would have realized he was slyly getting details.

It wasn't *her.* She wasn't special. This was simply a continuation of their two hot nights in Vegas.

When they reached her apartment, she tried to push the doubts and questions from her mind. A good thing, since the moment she closed the door, Gideon peeled off his jacket, shirt and tie, then pressed her against the wall. Within seconds, he had her skirt unbuttoned and pooled on the floor.

Her thigh-high stockings were certainly no barrier to his hands, and when he jerked at her panties, ripping the seams on one side, he groaned. "I want it all off, everything but the stockings."

"What are we doing?" she asked, the last vestige of sanity intruding.

"Screwing," he said, tossing her panties on the floor. "Well, about to, anyway."

"No, I mean this relationship, partnership, whatever. We're getting way too tangled up. You're solving a case, getting back your family's heirloom. I'm saving my job. Don't you think—"

"Do you really want to have this conversation *now?*"

She looked at him, so close, so hot and sexy. Her gaze skimmed his face, the focused look in his green eyes, his shaggy, mussed hair, then she let her gaze slide over his body, his tanned skin, the subtle ripple of muscle across his shoulders, chest and abs, the dusting of dark hair that arrowed down his chest, disappearing into the waistband of his pants.

She clasped her hand around the back of his neck and pulled his face toward hers. "Not really, no."

He fused their lips in a kiss almost brutal in its intensity. Her need for him exploded like a geyser. She couldn't get close enough, fast enough. She ripped at the waistband of his pants, then slid her hands down to shove them and his boxers past his hips. While he kicked them the rest of the way off, she attacked her suit buttons, and two of them popped off. When she managed to rid herself of the top half of her clothes, she reached for his erection, cupping his silky hardness in her fist. She wanted him inside her. She wanted the intimacy, the pleasure, the release, and she was sure her heart would jump out of her chest if that didn't happen in the next second.

He moaned against her throat. "Condom?"

Not wanting to let him go, she pumped his hardness. "Ah, my…my bag."

Kneeling, he fumbled in her purse for a minute, then stood with a foil packet in his hand. He ripped open the package with his teeth, then she snatched the condom from his hand and briskly rolled it on.

She would have liked to have tortured him by moving slower, but the itch he'd satisfied in the cab had roared back even stronger, and she wasn't in the mood for a slow ride to pleasure. She wanted him inside her, and she wanted him now.

He seemed to be of the same mind, since he immediately lifted her by the waist, bracing her weight against the wall. She wrapped her legs around his hips. He pushed inside her with a single, powerful stroke.

She gasped and closed her eyes, reveling in the sense of being filled, of the pulsing pleasure that rippled all the way through her body. *"Gideon…"* she whispered, his name both a plea and a sigh of appreciation.

As promised, he left on her stockings, and she found herself curious about the picture they made. When she'd danced, she'd always been conscious of the angles of her body, the way she needed to turn and move for the most sensuous effect. Tips paid the bills much easier than her salary, and the more popular she was with the customers, the more money she was able to demand from her employers.

It was all business.

She'd been mostly numb to the excitement she'd created and tried not to imagine the hard-ons she'd caused. It was easier, more tolerable, to do her job if she mentally distanced herself from the sexual aura on the stage and in the club.

Now, with Gideon moving against her, their bodies performing a sensual, powerful ballet, she finally understood why so many girls had gotten wildly turned on by their own performance.

Her hands braced against his shoulders, beaded with sweat, she rode his hips and the pleasure of him deep inside her, driving her against the wall. His breathing was labored, his muscles strained. She held on. She clung to him.

With the tightening tension low in her belly, the sense that her climax was just out of reach, she couldn't help but remember Vegas. That night she'd been lonely. He'd intrigued her, then satisfied a need.

Now everything was different.

The sex was good, maybe even better. But there was another layer now, a closeness and sense of togetherness that had been absent before.

She was a little scared by the difference. Even as she was fascinated.

Suddenly, Gideon increased his speed. His hands dug in to her bare butt. "Jacy, I—"

"Oh, boy," she moaned as the tension deep inside twisted another turn, then broke in a wave of pulsing bursts.

Gideon drove hard into her three more times, then his own climax broke. They bumped together, absorbing the moment, then they both slid weakly to the floor.

HIS BREATH HEAVING, Gideon rolled off Jacinda and onto his back. "I called you 'Jacy' again. Sorry."

She patted his shoulder. "It's fine. There was a whole déjà vu thing going on, huh?"

"I miss the slot machine."

"What for?"

He grinned, thinking about that tacky room where they'd spent the weekend in Vegas. "The ambiance, of course."

She propped herself up on her elbow and looked down at him. "You're joking."

"Yes." He brushed her tangled hair back off her face. "Your friend Patrick has much better taste in accommodations."

"The hot tub was nice, though."

"Yeah." Staring up at her, he lost himself in her beauty, her flushed face and bright blue eyes. It occurred to him that he could look at her for a long, long time and never tire of the sight. "We could fly down to my family's place in Bermuda one weekend soon. There's a great hot tub there."

Just like the last time he'd mentioned a trip away, a shadow passed through her eyes before she kissed him lightly, then rose to her feet. "Sure. Anytime."

She didn't believe they'd be together long enough for a tropical weekend getaway. Gideon could read that on her face as clearly as if she'd spoken.

He wanted to push. He wanted to assure her there was more, much more between them than a missing emerald and some good times between the sheets.

He glanced around at the strewn clothes. Okay. Maybe good times on the *floor*.

But it had been a long, emotional day, and he didn't want to break their tenuous peace. He'd have plenty of time to prove he was serious about pursuing their relationship.

"So, what are we—" He stopped as he spotted Jacinda standing a few feet away, the pictures of the emerald clutched in her hands.

So much for peace.

Her gaze jerked to his, her eyes narrowed in accusation. "Where did you get these?"

He didn't see any way to finesse a kind answer. "I took them with a camera the day you let me in the vault."

Anger tightened her face.

"I needed them for a gem expert," he continued, reaching for his pants, then sliding them on. Defending slightly unethical claims was probably better done dressed.

"No expert could tell you definitively about the emerald's characteristics from a picture."

"But the color's unusual, you know that. You read the testimony from people who've seen it. Not to mention the rarity of the size. My expert told me he'd be willing to say it was very probable that the Veros emerald had once belonged to my grandmother."

"Why didn't you show these to Pascowitz Friday?"

"I—" He realized now that his tendency not to show all his cards had probably saved her job. Pascowitz would have blamed her for the breach in security. Unfortunately, his ambition to get the emerald had blinded him to that possibility.

"Because I'd hoped I wouldn't need them." He refused to blink away from her frosty glare as he told her the rest. "And I wanted the expert's testimony in person. He was out of town on Friday. I arranged for him to come with me on Monday morning."

She paled. "Tomorrow?"

He reached for her hand, but she forced the stack of pictures into his, then walked naked down the hall. "I'm sorry," he said to her retreating back. "I should have told you sooner."

She stopped and glared at him over her shoulder. "No. You shouldn't have taken them at all." Then she stormed into her bedroom.

He followed and found her sliding into a silk robe, the same one she'd tossed on the bed while getting dressed when they'd left earlier.

He wasn't usually this inept at conciliation. Apologies were not his strong suit—he'd bet his grandmother had left that trait out of his gene pool—so he had to work extra hard.

"I'm sorry," he said. "The emerald is very important to me."

Meeting his eyes, her gaze was furious. "And you're willing to betray me to get it."

"No." He hadn't *betrayed* her. He'd simply pursued the most expedient means to the end. *His* end. "I just— I needed the pictures," he said, knowing his explanation sounded ridiculously weak.

"We have some lovely ones in our brochure."

"I needed my own. Close micro-shots. I needed to be sure all the details were covered."

"But you didn't *ask*," she said quietly, accusingly. "You just *took*." She closed her eyes for a moment, and when she opened them, they didn't reflect anger. They were filled with pain.

She crossed her arms over her chest. "You never considered the position these pictures would put me in. You never considered that anyone who saw them would classify them as surveillance.

"What else did you take pictures of? The guard station? The hallways and security panels? Maybe the air-conditioning vents?"

Gideon felt his own temper spike. "I didn't have anything to do with the break-in."

"So you've said." She lifted her chin. "I think you should leave."

He surged toward her, gripping her shoulders. "Damn it, I didn't take it!"

She looked away. "I'm tired. It's been a long day, and you need to go."

"Look at me!" Overwhelmed by the anger and fear coursing through him, he shook her slightly. "Do you think I took—or helped somebody else take—that gem?"

She stepped back. "Gideon, don't. Not now."

He refused to back down. They had something special together, but if she didn't believe in this basic tenet of his character, they had nothing. "Yes, now. I want to know. I *need* to know."

She sighed. "I don't *want* to believe you're responsible."

"That's not an answer."

She glared at him. "Well, that's the only one you're getting." She jabbed the center of his chest with her finger. "You lied to me in Vegas. You let me believe you were struggling and poor. You used our relationship from back then to get into the vault. Then you unloaded your big plan to get back the emerald, *supposedly* stolen from your grandmother, but, oh, you *conveniently* forgot to mention she doesn't really want it back. Then you suddenly have an in with the police department, and a father who's some kind of security expert. And every damn time I turn around, I find out something else you've kept from me, some other aspect to your grand plan that's a secret.

"So if all that sends me over the edge, I'm thinking you ought to pick up on my intense frustration." She advanced on him, backing him to the doorway. "And, by the way, I'm not really in the mood to hear about what *you* wanted and what *you'd* planned to do before this morning. Somebody's got that emerald, and—from my perspective anyway—you're looking like a pretty good suspect. So do you really want me to answer that question about whether or not I think you're guilty?"

He said nothing for a long moment, watching her, the exhaustion and frustration clearly stamped on her face. He considered her words, and the clear evidence of his selfishness from the moment he'd reentered her life. "No, I don't think I do." He turned. "I'll go."

"Great. Please do," she called as he walked down the hall.

Grabbing his shirt, jacket and tie, he flew out of the

apartment, dressing in the elevator. Pissed and disappointed with her but mostly himself, he took a cab to Midtown, stopped by the pub near his apartment and ordered a strong cup of coffee.

"Gideon, man, you look like hell," the bartender, Bobby, said, setting a cup in front of him.

"Perfect. I feel like hell."

"Gotta be a job or a woman."

Gideon swallowed a mouthful of coffee. "Worse. It's both."

"You wanna talk about it?" Bobby asked, leaning against the bar.

"Maybe later. I'm wallowing now."

Shrugging, Bobby wandered off.

Gideon cupped his mug and sighed. Why did he always have to forge his own path? Why hadn't he fully shared his plans with Jacinda? Why couldn't he take that next step and consult her *before* he moved ahead?

Maybe in the beginning they'd been awkward strangers-with-a-past, but they weren't anymore, and he'd had plenty of opportunities to be forthcoming. His need to stay in control, to dictate and have his own way, was messing up everything. Maybe he was trying to make it work with her, but he hadn't trusted her with his quest for his family heirloom, he hadn't put faith in their bond.

It was no damn wonder she was running in the other direction.

The more he thought about the past few days, the more certain he became that he was screwing up something rare and amazing. They worked together like a dream. She picked up on his cues. She understood his motivation and direction without him having to explain anything. Personally, her laughter warmed him deep in his soul. Her obvious desire for him made him feel strong and important. He wanted to touch her, protect her and enjoy her every minute of the day.

But when he found the emerald, when it was publicly claimed as Graystone family property once again, he'd be gone. On to the next adventure and challenge. He never stayed in one place too long. Someday he might expend the wanderlust, but for now he knew it was as much a part of him as breathing.

Jacinda was settled in the city. In Vegas, she'd told him when she finally made it to New York, when she finally had a place to belong, she'd never leave it.

Eventually, they'd move in opposite directions.

Maybe she was right. Maybe he needed to find his Vegas attitude again, to enjoy her for the moment, to hell with the complications and emotions. It was certainly simpler. Easier.

And since when have you ever taken the easy path? his conscience reminded him.

Before he could pursue that avenue of thinking, his cell phone rang. He reached into his suit coat pocket and glanced at the screen.

Jacinda.

His heart gave him one swift kick before he answered. "Hi."

"Don't talk," she said. "I just want to tell you one thing, then I'm going to bed. It's a big thing for me to admit, so you should feel damn lucky I'm so weak right now that I'm willing to babble."

"But I need to apologize—"

"No talking. Here it is." She drew a deep breath. "I

believe you didn't take the emerald. I believe you're a man who acquires treasures for honor and pride. I believe you, Gideon. I just don't want to."

Gideon waited for the rest, for an explanation of what that meant. Didn't he just say they were great at picking up on each other's cues? If so, he needed a teleprompter for this one. The believing in him part was nice, but everything else was a mystery.

"Jacinda?" he asked cautiously.

Nothing.

She was gone.

Gideon dropped the cell phone back in his pocket and hunched over his coffee mug.

10

On Monday, Jacinda spent the morning unpacking the last few items for the auction that somehow was only two days away.

She held a pair of jeweled opera glasses up to the light. She saw the flaws from a professional standpoint, but the glasses belonged to Malle Callibro, so they were nothing short of amazing. The family sometimes allowed Malle's possessions to be auctioned off, either for a good cause, or to draw attention to a particular auction. Jacinda was honored they'd chosen hers to highlight.

The auction house meant so much to them all—the family, their clients, the employees and especially Mr. Pascowitz. A week ago, she would have said it meant everything to her, but since seeing Gideon again, she had to admit she'd become curious about how the treasures found their way to the warehouse.

After the volatile way she'd grown up, she'd craved stability, and now that she had it, she wanted something more. Gideon, with his travels and passion, had sparked a sense of adventure and longing she'd never dreamed she possessed. She wanted to share that excitement with him. She wanted their wild nights to continue.

If she'd told him that, if he'd told her everything about

his plans, would they be in a different place now? Would she be beside him as his expert gemologist was, at this moment, giving his all-important testimony to her boss?

The fact that the ownership still mattered, when the gem in question was missing, only proved Gideon's commitment not to the emerald itself, but to its legacy, and made her feel even more regretful than she already did.

He certainly should have told her about the pictures he'd taken, but she'd overreacted to finding them. She'd dropped back on her old crutch—the past, where her mother believed every lover's empty promise, where Jacinda herself had learned to be distrustful and suspicious.

Setting aside the glasses, she pulled the next item from the box. She unwrapped it and found one side of a bronze, eagle-shaped bookend. As she glanced at her inventory sheet, she sighed. The list described a bear, not an eagle. That was going to be a problem.

Though considering one of their most prominent gems was currently missing and the police were still prowling around the building as if the thief and their missing inventory were both going to jump out from behind a display case at any moment, the issue of bear versus an eagle seemed slight.

She turned when the door opened, prepared to see one of the warehouse workers and ask him if he'd seen a bear bookend. Maybe there had just been a switch.

But Gideon appeared in the doorway. He glanced around briefly before spotting her, kneeling beside the box of treasures.

Wearing his standard uniform of faded jeans and a fitted T-shirt—this one in black—he walked toward her.

Watching him, the faint smile on his face, the casual but determined way he moved, the windblown disarray of his hair that made him look as if he'd just stepped off the deck of a ship, her heart jumped.

Oh, hell, I love him.

Her palms went damp. How had she possibly let *that* happen?

He knelt next to her and cupped her face in his hand. His gaze searched hers, his eyes warmer and more tender than they'd ever been. She found herself holding her breath.

Did he know about her feelings? Why did he have to be so intuitive? Why couldn't she figure out the art of the politely interested expression?

He angled his head. *"I believe you didn't take the emerald, but I don't want to?"*

She sighed in relief. He didn't know. Her rambling from the night before had confused him enough to distract him. "It's nothing. I was tired. Forget it."

"Can I focus on the believing-in-me part?"

"Sure."

"I'm sorry I haven't trusted you."

"It's okay. We're both too independent for our own good sometimes."

He pulled her to her feet and into his arms. "Well, I'm hoping to change that this morning. I changed my—" His eyes narrowed suddenly. "What's wrong?"

The confusion has cleared. "Nothing. Except I need a bronze bear bookend."

"Can't help you there." He grinned wickedly. "However, if you'd like to hire my special services to locate a particular bear, Ms. Barrett, my rates are very reasonable."

"Do I get the partner discount?"

"Naturally."

"How about you help me unpack the rest of my box, then we'll start our search."

He kissed her softly. "I'm all yours."

She smiled up at him even though her stomach sank. He wasn't hers at all. She might have his attention at the moment, but that wouldn't last.

While they finished unpacking and checking off the inventory, she managed to act normal, or at least as if she hadn't just had the greatest revelation of her life. It helped that Gideon told her stories about some of his adventures, including a six-month underwater exploration for a pirate's chest that turned out to be filled, not with gold, jewels or fascinating pieces of history, but cannonballs.

"Six months for lumps of lead?" she asked, incredulous. "Does that happen often?"

"No, thankfully. Though the foundation that footed the bill for the dives wasn't too comforted by that."

"So you paid them back."

"A bit."

"How much?"

She was pretty sure he was blushing. "Fifty percent. How do you know I paid them back?"

"It's something you'd do," she said simply.

He leaned close, his gaze roving her face before dropping to her lips. "I'm a pretty nice guy, huh?"

The hint clear, she smiled, then kissed him lightly. "You're pretty great."

When she would have pulled back, he grasped the back of her head and deepened the kiss. The hot rush of need that always accompanied moments with Gideon washed over her. The feelings she'd suppressed for the past hour rose to the surface again, making the moment seem more poignant for her.

He was an adventurer, a free—if wealthy—spirit bound for his next mission at any moment. His giving nature and ready-for-anything attitude were just a couple of the things she loved about him. But he couldn't imagine life without a nice, soft cushion of money. He couldn't understand her long-held need to climb the corporate ladder. He wouldn't ever be a business executive and wear serious blue suits— unless called to his grandmother's for dinner. And while she might be able to convince him to stay with her awhile, he might never be secure, at least not in the way a woman like her craved.

They weren't meant to be together.

They could just have fun in the meantime.

Gideon leaned back a bit, his lips curving mischievously. "So how many dark and private corners are there in this warehouse?"

"Several," she said, sliding her hand down his chest. "*However,* I'm working at the moment, and that sort of behavior isn't appropriate—"

He kissed her at the base of her throat. "I love it when you set up rules."

"You don't have rules, so why—"

The warehouse door, the one that led from the offices, opened then shut with a loud slam.

Jacinda jolted to her feet, smoothing the wrinkles from her pantsuit. Her job, her *dream* job, was in jeopardy, and she was making out instead of working. It was something her mother would do, so something she would never be tempted by.

And yet, here she was.

Within seconds, one of their warehouse attendants rounded the corner of crates stacked several rows deep and paused at the sight of her and Gideon. "Ms. Barrett?"

"Hi, Cal, where are we with the displays?"

"Comin' along," he said in his deep Southern accent, continuing to move toward her. "I could use that crate you've got there."

"I'm all ready for you." She turned to Gideon. "Cal, this is Gideon Nash. His family are patrons, and he's interested in some of our auction items."

Cal shook Gideon's hand, the relief on her fellow employee's face obvious. "Great to meet you, sir. You startled me at first, because all visitors are restricted, but I can see why Ms. Barrett made an exception in your case."

Jacinda didn't want Cal examining Gideon's family connections too closely, especially since he was about to claim one particular item as belonging to him, so she started toward the door. "We were just about to head back to my office, so these are all yours."

Thankfully, Gideon took the hint and followed.

"Okay, Ms. Barrett!" Cal called. "You just let me know if you need anything. Your first auction. It's a big, hootin' deal."

After she scanned her ID through the electronic lock, Gideon held open the door to the main hallway. "*Are* you nervous?"

Again, her mind zipped instantly to the new awareness of the feeling deep in her heart. "About what?"

"The auction." He grinned. "*It's a big, hootin' deal,* you know."

She waggled her finger at him. "Don't start. I need Cal. He's the hardest-working, most conscientious warehouse guy we have."

"I wasn't going to make fun. I think he's great. Colorful. A damn sight more interesting than most of the stiffs—"

"You'll change your tune if one of those *stiffs,*" she said, whispering the last word, "particularly Mr. Pascowitz, jumps to your side and gets you the emerald."

He gave her a half bow. "I most certainly will."

Without commenting, but dying to know how the meeting had gone, she headed down the hall toward her office. That charm got him whatever he wanted. Including her. Even Pascowitz wasn't immune to it. Gideon probably already had a signed statement of ownership in his pocket.

Things that came easily to people irked her.

But then he wouldn't actually have the stone itself. The thief had been very clever, and there was no reason to assume he wouldn't continue to be. Which probably meant Gideon would never get his hands on it.

He clearly didn't need the gem itself, though. Just the proof of who it belonged to. He wasn't going to hold it up for TV cameras, sell it to the highest bidder or laud his great achievement in getting it back. He'd just know it was his, in his heart.

How could she not love a man like that?

When she and Gideon reached her office, he closed the door behind him, and she turned to face him. "Did you get it?"

He looked confused. "What?"

"The emerald, what else?"

"Uh, Jacinda, the emerald's been stolen." He walked toward her, his expression concerned. "Are you feeling okay?"

"*Me?* Didn't you and your expert have an appointment with my boss this morning?"

"Oh, that. I cancelled."

Her jaw dropped. "*Oh, that?* When did you cancel? Are *you* okay?"

"I'm fine, but I was up late last night, so I'm a little—"

"Doesn't the emerald's ownership hinge on Pascowitz's recommendation to the board? Isn't the recovery of the stone the whole reason you're in the city?"

He grasped her shoulders, turning her toward her desk. A large box sat in the center. "It *was.*

"That's all the information I have on the emerald," he said from behind her. "Everything, including my notes, thoughts and suspicions, plus the police reports I managed to get from Santoni."

Her heart pounding, she glanced back at him. "Why?"

"I need your help. I've been over it dozens of times, and I don't know what to do anymore." He stroked his hand down her cheek. "I know you're busy, but I really need you to look through everything. I need to know if I'm right."

"About what?"

"Who took the emerald."

She searched his eyes, longing to ask why he'd cancelled his meeting with Pascowitz and the gem expert. She wanted him to tell her his theories. Most of all, she wanted to know why he was trusting her with something incredibly dear to him—his family.

But she asked none of that. There was a shadow of worry and sadness in his eyes she'd never seen before. He wasn't asking for help to coddle her or get back in her bed or good graces.

He was scared.

Even though she was worried about what he'd discovered that troubled him so much, she smiled, laying her hand over his for a moment of comfort before she started toward her desk. "The original thief, or the one who took the stone from our vault?" she said as she took off the cover of the box, trying to seem nonchalant, trying not to betray how much his trust meant.

Gideon sank into one of the chairs on the other side of her desk. "The most recent one."

She peered inside at the box's cherished contents, then lifted them out.

Gideon had organized the information by dates, so she pulled out a dry erase board and made a time line. With his help, they worked with concrete information first— copies of receipts, insurance reports, pictures and their own observations of the emerald and what had happened before and after it was taken.

Then they categorized the verbal information—people who'd actually owned the emerald, insurance adjusters who'd appraised it, pawnshop owners who'd sold it. Then they went with the stories of people who claimed they'd admired it at a party, seen it in a display case or heard from a friend's uncle's cousin about how it dazzled the crowd at some nightclub celebration.

More than two hours later, she gazed at Gideon across a sea of paper. She wanted to shake away the suspicion that had taken hold some time ago, the one that would hurt Gideon the most. But she knew delaying her thoughts wouldn't help.

"She took it," she said, still not entirely believing it herself. "Your grandmother stole her own emerald."

Gideon's eyes were bleak. He leaned forward, bracing his forearms on his thighs. "Yeah. I think so, too."

"I'M NOT SO SURE this is a good idea."

Gideon laid his hands around his coffee mug and shook his head. "We have to confront her."

Jacinda glanced around the elegant, busy restaurant— one of his grandmother's favorites. "Couldn't we do it someplace a little more private?"

"Where she can blow us off and continue to avoid the questions that need to be asked?" He shook his head again, then sipped his coffee. "No."

"Maybe we're wrong."

He glanced at her. "You think we're wrong?"

She bit her lip. "No."

The cautious nature still held at her core, the one not even Jacy Powers had been able to overcome. He wished she could see how brave and strong she was. He wished she could see herself as he did.

But she'd helped him. She'd trusted him even when he'd kept secrets from her. She'd believed in him.

That was something to build on.

Which they would do once this whole emerald business was settled. And that couldn't happen until he confronted his grandmother with his suspicions.

If what he and Jacinda alleged was true, he was going to have to do some slick talking and maneuvering to get them all out of this theft business unscathed. That had never been a problem before, but having his lover and a member of his family so intimately involved in one of his recovery operations wasn't an experience he wanted to repeat anytime soon.

His stomach was tied in knots, hence a splash of the Irish in his coffee. He wanted nothing more than to bury himself in Jacinda's arms and hope all this would go away.

Since that wasn't an option—and completely unlike him—it fell to him to keep Jacinda's spirits up.

"Trust me," he said, sliding his hand over hers. "It's all going to work out."

She jerked her hand back so fast she nearly turned over her water goblet.

"What's wrong?"

"Nothing," she said, then turned deathly white and took a big gulp of water.

Clearly, something was wrong. "Jacinda, please."

"People…" she began to say, then shook her head. "*Men* used to say that to my mother all the time. Usually right before they took off with her last hundred bucks."

He knew, from his own investigation and little clues from her, that her childhood hadn't been pretty. But she'd never given him many details.

"It's nothing." She clenched her hands together in her lap. "It's not important."

"Yes, it is. Tell me."

It was a moment before she spoke. "My mother was gullible. She always believed the next guy she met was on his way to being the next megamillionaire casino king. Within a few weeks, days or sometimes hours, she'd realize he wasn't. Somehow, though, she never came to her senses until after the jerk ran off with our rent money."

"I'm sorry," he said softly.

She didn't seem to hear him. "I told her thousands of

times that she could make her own fortune, or at least a
decent life, but she never listened. Every time a guy left,
I told her it wasn't her fault. I helped her pick up her pride
and move on. Then the next guy came along with empty
promises and a bright smile.

"I left when I was sixteen, and one of her boyfriends
came on to me. We didn't talk for years afterward. But I
called her eventually. She's my mother after all."

"Where is she now?"

"Still in Vegas. Still a cocktail waitress. Still looking
for her dream guy. Still—"

"Letting you bear the burden when she screws up."

Her gaze flicked to his, where he saw shame. "Yeah."

Her humiliation nearly broke his heart. "I'd do the
same thing."

"You wouldn't." She shook her head. "You—"

"I would. You don't get to pick your family the way you
do your friends. That's why it's even more important to
hold relationships together. You're supposed to."

She offered him a small smile. "Thanks, I—"

"Are you still expecting one more?" the waitress asked.

Gideon glanced at his watch. Gran was never more
than ten minutes late—just long enough to make a
dramatic entrance. "She should be here any moment."

"Can I get you anything else while you wait?"

"Some more water, please," Jacinda said, sounding
hoarse.

She *did* still look a bit shaky, and Gideon wasn't sure
if his words or his presence had really comforted her. The
deepest cuts took the longest to heal, and her mother's in-
stability had obviously left a serious wound.

I believe you, Gideon. I just don't want to.

Her words from the night before came back to him and suddenly made sense.

And that realization forced him, for maybe the first time, to appreciate how privileged he was. How fortunate he'd been, not only to have money and power at his disposal, but also to have his family's support. His mother, if she had any flaw, had been guilty of overindulgence, while Jacinda had not only been neglected by hers, she'd been saddled with the role of responsible adult. His mother had nurtured him and taught him empathy. His father had taught him strength and perseverance. How was it that Jacinda had all those qualities as well, but no one who'd guided her to them?

She was truly a remarkable woman.

Before he could find the right words to tell her that, his grandmother made her appearance. He'd chosen a restaurant where she was well-known, and one where, despite her constant assurances to the maître d' that she didn't need to be fussed over, she would indeed be fussed over.

"I'm fine, Armando, truly," she said as she glided toward them.

"Madame Graystone, please allow our sommelier to bring you a bottle of pinot noir. He keeps a few special selections in the cellar especially for you." The maître d' appeared as though he wouldn't move until he'd seen to her every need.

She sighed, so deeply and dramatically that even Jacinda's gloom disappeared. She held her hand over her mouth, and Gideon was sure she was stifling a giggle.

"Very well, Armando," his grandmother said with a wave of her hand while Armando nearly took flight in his haste to fetch the wine.

"She's amazing," Jacinda said, clearly in awe.

"She's something, all right," Gideon muttered as he stood and held out his hand. "Gran, how gracious of you to join us."

She angled her head, her face the picture of innocence. "Am I late?"

"Of course not, Mrs. Graystone," Jacinda said, sending Gideon a dark look.

"Please call me Sophia." Gran settled into the booth between them. "You are a lovely, gracious woman. What the devil are you doing with him?" she asked, jabbing her thumb in Gideon's direction.

"You're not helping, Gran," Gideon said. "I'm trying to convince her of my sterling character and reputation."

"That, I would think, is an entirely futile project." She gave him a pointed look. "But then wild-goose chases seem to be your specialty these days."

A man, presumably the sommelier, stopped next to the table, a bottle of wine tucked beneath his arm. With a ridiculous amount of ceremony, he tucked a stark white linen napkin around the back of the bottle and presented it to Gran. "The 2003 Kosta Browne Koplen Vineyard Russian River Valley."

"Do we have to pay by the word?" Gideon whispered, a bit loudly, to his grandmother.

The sommelier face's reddened, clearly thinking Gran wasn't happy with the selection.

"My grandson," Gran said with her usual grace and smoothness. "He's a bit uncouth at times. I blame it on a lack of culinary appreciation."

"Hey," Gideon said. "Just because I like that box wine…"

The sommelier's face turned white.

"Stop it," she said to him. To the sommelier, she bestowed a dazzling smile. "Please pour."

With another few minutes of unnecessary ceremony, the sommelier presented Gran with a cork and a small measure of wine to taste.

She swirled and tasted, and though Gideon could appreciate good wine as much as anybody, he appreciated more the speed with which he could get into the box wine and actually be drinking it. Thankfully, Gran pronounced the wine excellent, after which the sommelier poured three glasses.

As he walked away, Gideon commented, "Good grief. I could've shot two fingers of whiskey in that time."

"Then your tongue would have been numb, and you wouldn't be able to appreciate the fine dinner I'm treating you and Jacinda to."

Sitting back in the booth and enjoying his glass of wine, which *was* really good, it took a few seconds for the meaning behind Gran's words to penetrate. He'd insisted on this meeting to talk about a subject she clearly wanted no part of and now she was paying for dinner? "You're treating?"

"Yes. Unfortunately, I can't stay for dinner, darling. There's an emergency meeting at the garden club. Your mother's determined to have everything go flawlessly."

That woman had left smooth behind forty years ago. Now she was as glossy as the flawless diamond on her finger. "You're choosing the garden club over your grandson?"

"What kind of matriarch would I be if I didn't set the example and make necessary sacrifices?"

The superglossy kind who knows how to manipulate

every situation to her advantage. It was obvious he'd have to go the direct route. "Gran, you promised to talk to me about the emerald."

"Naturally, I will." She glanced at her watch. "I have twenty minutes."

"Good. That should be enough time for you to tell me why you took it."

Jacinda choked on her wine.

Gran widened her eyes. "Took what? Gideon, have you taken leave of your senses? I—"

"You stole that emerald. I know you did. Now I want to know why."

11

"LET'S HEAR IT," Gideon said when Gran just stared at him in silence.

"First of all, Gideon Michael, you'll change your tone. I'm your grandmother."

His gaze flicked to Jacinda, whose eyes held censure. She mutely shook her head at him, and he realized he'd let his anger get the best of him. But after all the years of searching for that blasted stone, of trying to regain his family's honor and right an old wrong, he'd been bested by the one person he'd hoped to impress.

"I apologize," he said in a softer voice. "I'm just disappointed."

Clearly upset, Gran sipped her wine. "That's very difficult to hear."

Jacinda leaned forward to speak to him around Gran. "Gideon, don't you think—"

"We have to know, Jacinda. You have to overcome the embarrassment of having one of your auction items stolen out from under you. I'm fighting to prove the emerald belongs to my family. How would it look if it's proven, or even suspected, that a Graystone stole it?"

"I didn't take it," Gran said.

"Semantics," he said. "You hired someone to take it."

"You are seriously overstepping your bounds, young man," Gran said, her eyes flashing with anger, and a hint of pain.

The stone had once meant a great deal to her, Gideon suddenly realized. His great-grandfather had bought it for Gran's tour of Europe. That had to have been a momentous occasion in her life. So what happened later? What had caused the pain? Who was she covering for?

This whole business was emotional for Gran, much more so than he'd ever anticipated.

"Please let me out," Gran said abruptly. "I need to go."

Gideon rose and helped her slide out of the booth.

Without a backward glance and leaving her wine virtually untouched, she stalked away from the table. Armando and the sommelier tried to chase her down, but she merely gave them a tight smile and walked through the door held open by a quick-thinking hostess.

"Sir," Armando said with a catch in his voice, "have we somehow offended Mrs. Graystone?"

"No." Gideon returned to his seat, feeling the weight of guilt and anger heavy on his heart. "She just received an urgent message from her daughter." He lifted his head long enough to try to offer a comforting smile to the two men hovering by the table. "The garden club fund-raiser is a particular passion to the family, and there are details that only she can see to. She expressed her sincere apologies to you both."

"And th-the wine, sir?" the sommelier asked hesitantly. "Does it meet with your approval?"

Jacinda slid her hand along Gideon's thigh. "It's wonderful, but Mr. Nash would prefer a drink just now. It's been a long day. Johnnie Walker Black, two fingers, neat."

The sommelier couldn't hide a brief moment of shock, but he recovered quickly, nodded, then backed away. "Of course."

"Are you trying to get me drunk?"

"Absolutely. I'm dying to take advantage of you."

He said nothing, though the echo of his own words from Saturday night gave him some comfort. At least Jacinda wasn't walking out on him, though the reason she was hanging around eluded him at the moment.

The waiter brought the drink, and Gideon stared at the amber liquid for a long time before taking a bracing sip. "I'm an ass."

"Maybe occasionally, but you're doing what you have to. You're right. We have to find out what's going on, or none of us can move on."

"I know." But the memory of the betrayed look on his grandmother's face would live with him long into the night. "We have to end this."

"How about we eat first?"

She called the waiter over, then ordered for both of them, obviously deciding he wasn't in any decent state to choose for himself. Their silent communication, their sense of each other's moods, was helpful once again.

During dinner, she talked about funny things that had happened at the auction house. He knew she was trying to cheer him up, and, though it didn't really work, he was glad she made the effort.

"And once," she said over dessert, "there was a guy who nearly got away with selling off a fake Degas. He had several certifications, which were, of course, forged. But Mr. Pascowitz thought his eyes were shifty, and his designer suit wasn't quite up to par."

"Snobbery finally comes in handy."

"Exactly. So Mr. P. called in his own expert to examine the painting, and while it was a very good copy, it was still a copy."

Gideon raised his eyebrows. "Sherman saved the day?"

"Everybody's entitled to one highlight."

He supposed they were. He paid the bill, and as they walked out of the restaurant, he started to hail a cab, but Jacinda pulled him down the sidewalk. "Let's walk a bit."

He glanced at her high-heeled pumps. "Those don't look like walking shoes."

"Then we'll go slowly."

She said nothing more until they reached the crosswalk at the end of the first block, where she squeezed his hand. "No matter what the truth is, you'll work it out with her."

"I don't know. I was pretty much a jerk."

"But you *have* to reunite."

"Why's that?"

"You're the optimist. I'm the pessimist. What will people think?"

He laughed and hugged her to his side. It felt good to share his disappointment with someone. Not just his parents, but with a…partner. He'd always been a loner and really never thought of himself any other way. Jacinda had changed that. She made him think about connections and bonds.

"And your family works through things," she continued. "*Any* thing. I can tell."

"How's that?"

"The way you tease each other and bicker, but there's love underneath."

"You and your mother love each other."

"Need, maybe. I don't know about love."

How incredibly sad was that? "That's not the way it's supposed to be."

"I know."

"It's not your fault. Nothing's lacking in you that makes her act the way she does."

"I know that, too." She smiled ruefully. "Sort of."

She needed somebody to love her and to love in return. Somebody deserving, strong and supportive. She didn't need a few nights of fun, empty promises or a fly-by-night adventurer like him. She needed—and deserved—something much more.

Jacinda looked up at him. "I know you feel bad about the *way* you said things to your grandmother, but do you still believe she took the emerald?"

He struggled to focus on the conversation instead of his disturbing thoughts. "I know it for sure now."

"Because of her reaction?"

"Yes. If she hadn't been responsible, she would have laughed me off. In fact, she probably would have added something about only a granny from the Graystone family could be that crafty at her age. Instead, she—" He stopped, thinking of the angry, pale expression on his grandmother's face. "Well, you saw her."

"I agree she acted guilty, and our own instincts certainly led us there, but *why* do you think she took it? It belongs to her in the first place. Why wouldn't she let you prove your claims, then get it back?"

"I don't think she wants it. Somehow, it reminds her of something painful from her past."

"Just so you're aware," she said dryly. "I'm not

planning to break in to any casinos anytime soon to get back any of my old costumes."

"I don't know…that silver one with the purple sequins in all the right places…"

She swatted him lightly on the arm. "Dream on."

Didn't the fact that she was making fun of her former profession show she was learning to accept her past? He was sick of seeing shame and regret in her eyes.

He looked left as the traffic stopped to be sure no errant, rushing taxies decided to challenge the light. "I know it sounds weird," he said, going back to his grandmother's grand crime, "to steal something you don't want, but that's the only thing that makes sense."

"If you say so."

He tugged her to a halt in front of a shoe store window. "You believe me."

"Sure. Why—" She stopped, her gaze connecting with his, the wording obviously not lost on her. Her eyes turned smoky and needy the way they did when she was aroused. But there was more this time, something else lingered beneath the fathomless blue. "You know her best, right?"

Confused, he kept his gaze on hers. He'd been so sure she was about to say more. But was he the right man to say anything more to?

"So what do we do now?" she asked. "We can't go to the police. Lieutenant Capshaw's tendency to be fair toward everybody isn't an advantage anymore. We *need* preferential treatment. Your cop buddy Santoni can't protect her and—"

He laid his finger against her lips. "What we do now is simple. We steal it back."

DRESSED IN A BLACK warm-up suit and running shoes, Jacinda glanced at her coconspirator across the backseat of the cab. "I can't believe you talked me in to this."

"Me?" Gideon glanced down at his navy T-shirt and jeans. "You're the one who looks like a cat burglar."

Jacinda glanced quickly at the rearview mirror, where the cabbie's interested gaze met hers. *Good grief, not again.* "I can't believe we're taking a cab," she said to Gideon.

"Would you prefer the subway?" he asked with maddening calm.

"Don't be ridiculous." She glanced anxiously out the window. At 2:00 a.m. even the traffic in Manhattan had lightened. They would be there in no time. "We should have rented a car, or a van, or…something."

"Maybe I should call James Bond and see if I can borrow his gadget-filled Aston Martin."

She turned her head and refused to look at him. What were they doing? What was *she* doing? If, by some miracle, her boss didn't find out about her scantily-clad-dancer past and fire her, she was going to get caught stealing a multimillion-dollar emerald—that had already been stolen once, maybe twice—from a prominent New York socialite and be tossed in jail.

Then she'd get fired *and* prosecuted.

"We can't do this," she said, her heart hammering as the possible scenarios and consequences zipped through her mind.

"It's my apartment," Gideon said. "What could happen?"

She crossed her arms over her chest. "Oh, your name's on the deed, is it?"

"It belongs to the family."

"We can't just waltz in there and take—" she glanced at the cabbie again and lowered her voice "—take back the *you-know-what.*"

Gideon's eyes danced. "The you-know—"

Jacinda shook her head quickly, pointing at the cabbie.

Gideon simply scooted beside her and whispered in her ear, "Think the cab's bugged?"

"This isn't funny," she whispered back, starting to really get angry. "This isn't right. We're breaking the law."

"No one will know."

"No one will know? *That's* your justification for this? What about your parents? And McElvy?"

He glanced at his watch. "My parents spend the week at their house in the Hamptons. McElvy and Gran go to bed at ten-thirty every night. She's become an early riser in the past few years. Don't worry. I'll take care of—" He stopped, seeming to realize he'd said the wrong thing.

They were *supposed* to be partners. At the very least, they'd earned each other's directness and honesty.

He laid his hand on her knee. "When we stop, I'll explain my plan, then you can plug all the holes. Agreed?"

"Agreed," she said, a bit grudgingly.

Maybe he was consulting her, but she had no doubt that if she hadn't agreed to come, he'd still be in this cab, going to the same place, doing the same illegal—possibly unforgivable—thing. And if she were Sophia Graystone, and she discovered her grandson had betrayed her in the way he was about to, she'd kick his ass from Park Avenue to the Bronx.

When the cab rolled to a stop, Jacinda scooted toward the door. "We're rehearsing for a play," she said to the cabbie's interested reflection before she exited the car, several blocks from Sophia's luxury apartment.

"Whatever you say, lady."

On the sidewalk, standing in the quiet, she fought to swallow her guilt. This whole thing was a bad idea. She could feel it in her bones as easily as she could appreciate the soft breeze that brushed her face, welcome in light of the summer heat. The bright green leaves on the trees in the park across the street fluttered. Maybe she could convince Gideon to take a leisurely walk instead of stealing a 21.4-karat emerald.

As the cab pulled away into the night, Gideon faced her. "We're going in through the front door. I have a key and the alarm code. Her safe is in the library. I know the combination for that, too."

He'd told her this hours ago, when she'd initially argued about the plan and they'd waited for the clock to tick by before they did the deed. Of course they'd passed the time by doing another, more sensual deed, during which she'd imagined herself as a character from a spy novel, which had *somehow* led to her donning the black warm-up suit and being led out to a cab at two in the morning.

"You're sure the emerald is in the safe?"

"Nearly sure."

Nearly sure. She was staking her entire future on *nearly sure.* She was tempted to bang her head against the nearest lamppost. "But why are you taking it? Why do you think this is the only way?"

"This will force my grandmother to tell me what's going on."

"Maybe. But remember how you felt at dinner, how you regretted what you said to her."

"I regretted how I *presented* it to her." He paced away, then back to her. "Jacinda, I can't get past this, my family can't get past this, until we know the truth."

"But what if—"

He clenched his fist as he jutted out his chin. "I've spent ten years of my life looking for that damn stone, and I think she owes me an explanation of what happened to it! Not to mention the jeopardy she's put you and the auction house in, or the trouble she's caused the cops. We deserve to know."

"Maybe we do, and maybe I don't appreciate what she's done, but a woman has the right to her privacy. If you're right, and this stone has caused her pain and embarrassment, I don't see why we can't just let it go."

He leaned close to her, his expression fiercely angry. "You think the cops are going to let it go? You think the auction house, their board of directors and the insurance company who hold the policy for the Veros family is going to *just let it go?*"

She'd never seen Gideon this way, so angry, so unwavering. And she couldn't help but worry that their actions might cause an irreparable rift in his family, a betrayal that neither their teasing or laughter could overcome. It would kill her to be part of such a thing.

She clutched his hand. "I just want you to pause a second and think. Think about what we're about to do, the confidence we're going to betray. This isn't the time to brashly jump forward."

He squeezed her hand, then paced away. "No? It certainly feels like it."

"You're sure this isn't a power game between you and your grandmother?"

"No." He paced back and forth along the breadth of the sidewalk several times, then he stopped and sighed. "Maybe it is."

"You want something. She doesn't want to give it to you."

"And without reasonable explanation."

"Not reasonable to you."

"You're making way too much sense."

She smiled. "I'm so glad." She walked toward him, laying her hands on his chest. "But so are you. I can't go back to work at the auction house and face everybody who's looking for the stone, knowing *I* know where it is. And you're right. There's no way she can keep this secret forever. Finding that emerald is too important to too many people."

"This is the only way."

She nodded. "One last chance for sanity—we could go back to my apartment. I'm sure we can think of *something* else to do besides breaking and entering."

For once, though, Gideon didn't seem interested in talking about sex. His eyes were shadowed with worry. "We have to get it back for her own good."

"I agree, though that logic might not go over well at next Sunday's dinner."

He grinned a bit wickedly. "And maybe I like the idea of taking something I shouldn't have."

She angled her head. "Is there a secret ambition to be a law-breaking outlaw you want to tell me about?"

"Mmm, well…" He wrapped his arm around her waist and guided her down the sidewalk—*toward* his grandmother's apartment building. "Did I ever tell you about the time I met Santoni crawling out a two-story window?"

She whipped her head toward him. "Ah, no. I think that one slipped by me."

"See, there was this woman…"

"Big shock."

"She might have been a striking brunet."

"I'll bet."

"Anyway, she wanted me to get back her diamond-and-ruby tiara. It had been lost during the settlement of her great-aunt's estate several years before. So, being from a prominent Boston family, she retained the services of my firm to recover the crown."

"Which you did."

"Naturally." He squeezed her side, and she felt the jolting spike of her pulse. "But then her check bounced."

"No. Seriously, her check bounced?"

"Yep. So, I do a little digging and find out that though my client does *resemble* Marie Edwards from Boston, the *real* Marie is on a yacht vacationing in the South Seas."

"But you'd already delivered the tiara to her."

His face flushed, and she wondered just how *striking* this brunet had been. "I had."

"So you had to get it back."

"Through her second-story apartment window. I, ah, *invited* myself in after midnight and helped myself to the tiara."

"Then met Sergeant Santoni at the bottom of the stairs."

"It was definitely a hairy moment, but I negotiated my way out of a jail cell and made a friend."

"And got the tiara."

He drew his shoulders back. "Which I returned to the Edwards family immediately. They were extremely appreciative of my integrity, since it was true that the crown had been lost for many years. They insisted on giving me a generous fee, which Gran made me donate to St. Peter's Orphanage."

"And Marie—the real one—was extremely grateful."

"She was."

Probably, she should be jealous. "I can't imagine any situation you can't negotiate yourself out of."

"You might be about to."

Jacinda's heart hammered with an odd kind of excitement. "But you've done this before."

Gideon craned his neck back to look up at the elegant brick-and-stone residence and seemed to realize the importance of their intent at last. "Not exactly."

GIDEON PAUSED outside his grandmother's apartment door.

Pausing and second-guessing his instincts weren't his thing. Was that Jacinda's influence, or were his actions really that weighty?

A few years ago, hell, a few *months* ago, he wouldn't have considered the opinion of a lover beyond her favorite flower, movie or choice of restaurant. Now, he wouldn't consider making a move regarding the emerald without consulting Jacinda. He wanted her opinion. He needed her support and encouragement.

What was he going to do when he had this case worked out, and he moved on to the next?

"You said you knew the code." Even though she whispered, her words echoed down the empty hallway.

He glanced back at her, cheered by the glittering interest in her eyes. Maybe they weren't as far apart as they'd first seemed. Maybe she wasn't as disinterested in his lifestyle as she'd once been. "I do. You remember the rules?"

"Stay right behind you. No talking. If I hear anything, I get still like a statue and not run like a rabbit."

He kissed her lightly. "The perfect student."

"Can I ogle your butt?"

"If it's absolutely necessary."

"I think it might be."

He turned to the keypad with his heart lighter and a smile on his face. She'd felt his nerves and eased them with a few words. He'd never been that in tandem with anybody.

His fingers seemed to glide over the numbers, the low series of beeps the only sound as he turned the doorknob and stepped across the threshold of Gran's apartment. The elaborate, overhead chandelier was dark, only a recessed bulb above the entryway painting provided any light.

The hushed, dark setting only heightened Gideon's senses—and his guilt. This was the right thing to do, the only way to force his grandmother to admit her role in the theft, to bring an end to sixty years of speculation and secrets and release Jacinda and the auction house from the scandal. Still, he hated doing this to his grandmother.

It occurred to him at that moment that he was hurt Gran hadn't come to him directly with her concerns. Sure, she'd tried to discourage him from proving the Graystone ownership of the emerald, but she'd done so casually, with a low-key cleverness that almost always worked. She hadn't anticipated his desire to punish those who'd taken advantage of her, and he hadn't anticipated how far she'd go to keep her secrets.

Shaking aside regrets and second-guessing, he crept down the foyer toward Gran's library.

He and Jacinda had shared champagne with her just the

night before. Despite the fact that he'd come here to pump Gran for information, they'd been relaxed and enjoyed each other's company. Now, he was turning the knob slowly, oh so carefully, then silently moving down the stairs and across the room, which was lit only by the desk lamp.

He was protecting his family even as he was betraying them.

Feeling only the heat of Jacinda's body behind him and the pounding of his own heart, Gideon moved to the back corner of the room. His feet didn't make a sound on the plush carpeting. He took a deep breath as he knelt in front of the bookcase, pressing the second book on the second row, which wasn't a book at all but a button that released the front of the case, revealing the safe beyond.

"That's—"

He reached back and grabbed her hand, silently urging her to go quiet. Timing and swiftness was critical. If McElvy rolled over and felt any sense of unease, if Gran headed to the bathroom, if either one of them decided to go for a frickin' glass of water in the kitchen, Gideon and Jacinda were screwed.

He knelt in front of the safe, then turned the dial. Even that slight movement and noise seemed to echo through the high-ceilinged room. His heart pounded, and a bead of sweat rolled down the side of his face.

Even though this was personal, even though this was like no other case before, the excitement never wavered. This was the reason he loved his job—such as it was. He admired Jacinda's professionalism and dedication to the auction house, but he could never work in an office, filling out forms and going to meetings, even if he had the access to the lovely treasures she did.

When the lock didn't give the first time, he assumed his distracted thoughts had led to the mistake. But when it didn't work the second, or the third, he realized the problem was much worse.

"She's changed the combination," he whispered in disbelief.

"She changed it?" Jacinda whispered back, her concern evident.

"The combination has always been my birthday. I'm her favorite grandchild."

"Don't you know how to crack it?"

He turned to stare at her over his shoulder. "No, I don't know how to crack it."

"In those spy movies, the hero *always* knows how to do stuff like that."

"Remind me to ask for a rewrite of our script."

The overhead light flipped on, and Gideon jolted to his feet.

Standing in the doorway was Gran, dressed in an immaculate rose pantsuit, looking as though she was expecting them. She raised her eyebrows. "I guess this means you're no longer the favorite."

12

THIS CAN'T BE GOOD.

Gideon reached for and found Jacinda's hand. He needed something to hold on to while his heart was falling to his shoes.

"I'd call McElvy for champagne," Gran said, walking down the steps toward them, "but I think we could all use something a bit stronger. Jacinda, do you drink whiskey?"

She squeezed Gideon's hand, and he could feel the sweat on her palms. "I do."

Gran made a sweeping motion with her hand. "Please, join me."

They did. They sat on the sofa, while Gran occupied her chair, just as they had the night before. Gideon simply held his glass and stared into it, the bizarre reality of what he'd done, what was happening now, rolling over him.

Had he permanently damaged the relationship with the person he respected above all others?

"Don't be so hard on yourself, darling," Gran said as if she'd read his thoughts. "I might have done the same myself once upon a time if somebody had stood between me and my goal."

"It wasn't like that. I—"

"He was protecting you," Jacinda said, her gaze locking with Gran's.

"He was, was he?"

"Yes," Jacinda said, seemingly undaunted by the challenge in Gran's voice. "You've committed a *felony*. You violated the security of a place I love dearly. You have the entire staff worried that some policeman is going to drag one of us away in handcuffs at any moment. You have the police questioning everybody they can get their hands on. You took something from the Veros family, who are kind and loyal people, who did nothing to deserve any of this."

Gran, instead of drawing on the significant heat and fury in her blue blood, simply angled her head as if Jacinda was an odd curiosity. "You seem like such a levelheaded young woman." Her exact words at the restaurant, though spoken in an entirely different tone this time. "Do you really believe I hired someone to steal that emerald? That, even now, it's sitting in my safe, just a few feet away?"

Jacinda's throat moved as she swallowed, but she didn't flicker as much as an eyelash as she said, "If Gideon says it's there, then it is."

"You believe I'd cause all this trouble for a piece of rock, one I could buy a hundred times over if I chose?"

"I believe Gideon."

For some weird reason, that made Gran smile. And while he appreciated Jacinda's defense and her unwavering belief in him over someone he knew she admired greatly, he didn't think now wasn't the time to challenge Sophia Graystone. Something strange was going on with her, and the less said at the moment, the better.

He kept a tight hold on Jacinda's hand and tried desperately to remember he was supposed to be the optimist.

"Well, I certainly never intended to cause all this trouble," Gran said calmly as she rose and walked toward the safe. "I would have found a way to compensate the Veros family. I would have made a generous donation to the auction house and a police charity, and I *never* would have allowed anybody to be arrested." She returned to them holding a black cloth bag, which she laid in Jacinda's lap. "Go on. Open it, then I'll explain. I can't have you two continue to look at me with such disappointment."

Jacinda set aside her glass, then reached inside the bag, and when she pulled out her hand and opened her palm, the emerald lay glistening against her fair skin.

After a moment, Jacinda's gaze slid to his, obviously searching for his reaction. Oddly enough, he felt no joy or satisfaction. He felt a dull kind of acceptance and, yes, disappointment.

Gran sighed as if she was disappointed in herself as well. "I never wanted to see that thing again, which is a shame, because I once loved it so." Her gaze moved to his, then to Jacinda. "I suppose I could say it's mine and, therefore, I didn't actually steal it. But that's a poor excuse, so I won't take that road. I've caused both of you a lot of grief, and I'm sorry about that. I truly am."

Gideon started to rise. He couldn't have her take all the blame. If he'd only listened when she tried to tell him to leave it alone. "No, Gran, you can't—"

She held up her hand. "Let me finish. Maybe sharing it will make it less painful." She linked her hands in her lap around her whiskey glass and stared in the distance, obviously into the past. "On that fateful trip to England, I wasn't as thrilled about meeting the King or wearing the emerald, I was excited to see a man. I'd met him at a party several months before when he'd come to New York with a friend. He was charming, handsome and elegant. And that accent..." She sighed lustily.

Watching his grandmother get hot and bothered over some English dude from her past was a strange experience. Who cared how a guy *talked?* But he noted Jacinda smiling, too, and figured it was another one of those female things that men would never fully understand.

"We were in England for a month, so Richard and I were able to spend a lot of time together. We went for walks in Hyde Park, visited museums and talked about everything. We fell in love, and we became lovers. My first, of course."

Gideon felt slightly nauseous and set his untouched glass of whiskey aside. "Ah, Gran, I don't really need to hear the details about that."

Jacinda nudged him. "Be quiet. I do."

"Obviously, it didn't turn out well," Gideon pointed out, already suspecting this English jerk of stealing the emerald. "And thinking about my grandmother..."

"All flushed and naked," Jacinda finished.

Gideon closed his eyes and shook his head. "Stop. Please stop."

"You two are so adorable," Gran said. "If only Richard and I had been so connected. But, as Gideon had guessed, things didn't turn out well. On our last night in London, he snuck into my hotel room, and we spent the night in my bed. He promised me he'd come to New York as soon as he could. He promised we'd marry and live happily ever after. He loved me, and he said he thought I was the most beautiful woman in the world when I'd worn the emerald necklace for the King. So I gave it to him. Something to remember me by."

Gideon resisted the urge to tug at his hair. "You *gave* it to him? A million-dollar necklace? Why couldn't he remember you with a picture? Or a lock of hair?"

"I was young and reckless." She lifted her eyebrows. "Surely you know what that feels like."

Gideon felt his face heat. "Maybe."

"I believed in him," Gran continued, her eyes sad as her gaze moved to Jacinda. "I believed he'd bring it with him to New York. I believed I'd wear it on my wedding day."

"Instead, a few weeks after I returned home, I saw Richard's friend, who told me Richard had turned out to be a cad, had stolen money from him and they were no longer associated. I told him he must be mistaken, that Richard would never do such a thing, but he told me that I shouldn't go near the man. He said that Richard wasn't a gentleman. He'd bragged about bedding some girl from the States, then pawning the necklace she'd given him."

"Oh, Sophia," Jacinda said, her eyes glistening with tears.

"I called the pawnshop for confirmation, of course, and learned the story was true. The pawnshop owner had already resold the necklace, and he wouldn't reveal to whom. I didn't care and was happy to never see it again. I'd been telling my parents the necklace was tucked in my drawer, but eventually they realized it was missing. I lied and told them I'd lost it the last night in England. Being careless was preferable to being stupid, you see."

Gideon had tracked the necklace back to its source accurately, but he felt none of the satisfaction he usually did. "Then my quest brought back all those terrible memories."

She nodded. "At first, I was sure you'd drop it. Then I was sure you'd never get enough proof to back up the claim, even if you did find it."

"At least until the Veros family decided to auction it," Jacinda said quietly.

"Exactly," Gran said. "Gideon, when you showed up here a few weeks ago, and you had that look in your eye, the one you no doubt inherited from me, I knew you'd never let it go." She sipped her whiskey. "I'm a proud woman. Maybe too proud. My reputation means everything to me. I couldn't let the real story come out. I couldn't face that humiliation again. I couldn't let you think I was a stupid, foolish woman. How would you ever respect me again?"

"I'll always respect you, Gran," Gideon said gently, rising to kiss her cheek.

He left her side and walked around the room, letting the story roll around his brain, letting the implications of her actions and his sink in. He understood pride—heaven knew he did—but would he really go to such extremes to protect his reputation?

He honestly wasn't sure, and it hardly mattered. She had, and now it was up to the three of them to figure out how to repair the damages. To everyone—especially his and Gran's special bond of love and trust.

"How did you find the thief you hired?" he asked his grandmother.

If she was surprised or offended by his brisk tone, she hid her reaction well. "Your father—"

"*My* father? Colonel Thurston Edward Nash put you in contact with a *thief?*"

She rolled her eyes in exasperation. "Oh, good heavens, let me finish. Impatient as a rabbit. You don't get *that* from me."

Suddenly, Gideon knew they were going to be okay. Whatever each of them had done, in their own stubbornness, they would find a way to reconnect. He'd told Jacinda families stuck together. Surely she was entitled to see the proof.

"Your father," Gran began again, "gave me the name of a man who used to work in Special Forces. I told him I needed a speaker for the Ladies' Veterans Auxiliary. Somebody who used to be dark and dangerous, I said. But one who could handle little old ladies gently. So, I met my…ah, contact, and told him my story."

"Hold it." Gideon raised his hands. "You told *him* about the necklace and Richard, being humiliated and so on, but you couldn't tell *me?*"

"How else could I convince him to help me?" she asked as if he'd missed the obvious. "He used to be a spy and assassin for the government, so he's quite intuitive. He'd have known if I was lying."

He glanced at Jacinda and noticed that she didn't look worried or angry, as she should. Instead, she seemed to be amused. She'd been as adversely affected by the theft as anyone, fearing for her own reputation and job, being interrogated by the police. That she could so easily accept his grandmother's reasoning was either a testament to her strength or, maybe, her faith in him.

He leaned toward her and kissed her full on the lips. "Thanks."

She touched his cheek. "For what?"

"Sticking with me."

"I also appreciate your support and discretion, Jacinda," his grandmother said, sounding as cheery as if they were talking about a party Jacinda had helped organize. Or maybe it was the whiskey. "Gideon hasn't always had the greatest judgment regarding women."

Gideon straightened and stared at Gran. "You were telling us about your government assassin and would-be thief…"

She pursed her lips. "*Former* assassin."

Gideon nodded. "Of course."

"Anyway, my hired man listened to my story and agreed to take on my case."

"For a hefty fee," Gideon said.

"*You* charge a hefty fee," Gran said, clearly annoyed. "Does that diminish the quality of your services or bring your motives into suspicion?"

He grinned. "Sharp as ever, Gran." Even in the middle of the night, after an extremely stressful few days and couple of belts of whiskey. He, on the other hand, hadn't even touched his drink but still felt the need for an aspirin and a nice, long nap. "Your thief agreed to divert a very sophisticated security system and steal the emerald."

"And nothing else." Gran waggled her finger. "This was critical. I was already compromising my integrity. I didn't want anything else to turn up missing."

Gideon exchanged a glance with Jacinda and knew she was thinking the same thing he was. "I'm sure the police appreciate your thief's reticence. However, the fact that he took just one thing was intriguing, *way too intriguing.* The fact that he compromised an extremely sophisticated security system has grabbed a lot of attention. Solving such an interesting case could make careers. I showed Jacinda's boss my evidence regarding the emerald's ownership. It would have only been a matter of time before the police would be knocking on our doors. The media has already leaped on the story. Your thief, as smart as he is, should have realized all that."

"He *is* smart. And—" she flushed "—he's quite charming. We have excellent chemistry."

"Oh, Gran."

"Your grandfather's been gone a long time. Why can't I flirt with a younger man?"

Jacinda giggled.

Gideon sighed. "No reason. No reason at all." He narrowed his eyes. "How young?"

"I have no idea, and it would be indiscreet to ask."

The guy was probably his dad's age. He didn't even want to think about somebody his *own* age, not that he would put that past her. The fact that he was a younger man was enough. A younger man who had experience as an assassin and a thief. He made a mental note to get the guy's name and do a full background check on Mr. Young-and-Charming ASAP.

"Don't worry about anything, Gran," he said, moving toward her to kiss her cheek again. "I'll take care of it."

Seeming to realize the party was over, Gran rose and walked him and Jacinda to the door. "What are you going to do?"

He lifted Jacinda's hand, which held the black bag containing the emerald. "Return this in time for the auction. That should satisfy everybody, including the police."

He was drained and not thinking clearly enough to come up with a plan at the moment. And while he was optimistic about getting everything to work out, after ten years of searching for the emerald, it was going to be hard to let it go.

As he walked out the door, his grandmother called to him. "I changed the safe combination to your cousin Alfred's birthday. You have a lot of work to do to get your favored status back."

Alfred. What a jerk. Just because he managed Gran's money, he thought he was a king.

Gideon sighed. "How about if I get the emerald back to the auction house, drop my mission to claim it as ours and make sure nobody gets blamed for stealing it?"

Gran raised her chin. "That's a good start."

Gideon said nothing during the elevator ride down to the street. So much had happened the past few days, he had no clarity about anything. His relationship with his grandmother, his relationship with Jacinda and his own view of himself all needed examining. He'd come to a place in his life where he couldn't just leap forward on instinct or solve his troubles with a smile and a phone call.

Pressure and stress, two things he avoided with incredible passion, had arrived at his door, unavoidable and looming.

"How are we going to make that all happen?" Jacinda asked as they climbed into the cab. "Getting the emerald back undetected, getting the police to drop the case."

"I have an idea, but it seems too simple to work."

"What's the plan?"

"We'll apologize."

"To who?"

"Everybody." He laid his hand on her thigh. "Can we work out the details tomorrow? The auction isn't until the day after." Right now, all he wanted to do was hold Jacinda, breathe in her coconut-and-sea scent and lose himself in her body.

She laid her hand on top of his. "Tomorrow's fine. But you do realize this case is over. You'll be moving on to the next mission soon."

You'll be leaving.

He heard her unspoken question. It was completely valid.

He was sure he'd feel the call to adventure again, but he wanted Jacinda, too. How he could convince her to come with him or his own heart to finally settle? Would one have to suffer to have the other? What if—he suppressed a shudder—he had to work in an *office?* Some of the time. A *little* of the time?

Jacinda was worth that. Watching her defend him tonight had been way more amazing than finding the Diamond of Sierra, or the stolen Picasso for Gran's high school friend or recovering any of the countless treasures he'd held in his hands.

All of those things combined didn't measure up to the emotions that rose inside him whenever he looked at the stunning woman next to him.

He pulled her close, his gaze on those luscious lips. "I'm not going anywhere tonight."

13

"THIS IS *WORP Channel Fourteen reporter Trish Sellers with an incredible wrap-up to the recent theft of the twenty-one-point-four-karat emerald recently stolen from Callibro's Auction House in Manhattan.*

"*While there may be no honor among thieves, there certainly seems to be remorse. Police recovered the emerald, which will be auctioned off later today, after a member of the auction house's cleaning staff found the valuable emerald inside a plain brown bag and sitting just inside the front door. The note inside simply said, 'I'm sorry. I regret taking something that wasn't mine.'*"

Sitting beside her desk, Jacinda lifted the remote to turn off the TV.

The plan had been way too simple, but it had clearly worked. With a little help from her and Gideon, of course.

She'd trusted Gideon to tell Pascowitz that his grandmother had found her emerald, so he was dropping his ownership claims. She'd agreed that returning the gem had to be anonymous and the less said, the better.

He'd trusted her that the head of the auction house's nighttime cleaning staff had irreproachable integrity, so that no one else would come under police scrutiny for the theft. He'd agreed that the low-key paper sack was the way to go.

Since the recovery of the emerald early that morning, the board of directors had congratulated Mr. Pascowitz on his impressive leadership, and her boss, for once, had given partial credit to someone else. Her. Jacinda didn't fear being fired; she anticipated being promoted.

The police, while disappointed they hadn't made a splashy arrest, had given sober interviews, then retreated to the station house, pleased to close the case. Lieutenant Capshaw had called her a few minutes ago, congratulating her on getting back the emerald, though she had suspected he knew there was more to the theft than what was obvious.

Sophia had also called that morning to thank her for handling everything with such discretion, class and smarts.

Jacinda knew Gideon was disappointed about letting the emerald go, but overall, everything should be great. She knew she should be happy, but she wasn't.

Gideon was gone.

After returning the emerald and holding their own, intimate celebration the night before, he'd clearly decided to move on. She'd found a note, a damn *note,* on the pillow next to hers that morning. She would have thought he'd written it at the same time he had the one from the "thief" had she not been there to help word the thief's remorse herself.

Gideon had apparently gotten an e-mail about a lead on a gold-and-diamond pipe that he'd been hired to find several months ago. He had to fly to Paris and didn't know how long he'd be gone. Be back soon, he'd said.

Please.

She'd known the man was going to break her heart, and he had. Why was she surprised? Why was she disappointed? She'd put her faith, love and belief into someone else, and he'd crushed her.

"It has been the weirdest week," Andrew said, leaning against her desk.

"Hasn't it?" she said, fighting for a light tone.

"But it all ends today."

How true.

"Speaking of weird..." Andrew began, leaning close to her. "You look weird."

"Gee, thanks. This suit cost a week's pay."

"Not like that. The suit is perfect. Red is your color, bolder than your usual neutrals and pastels." He brushed his hands down his magenta jacket, which had made Jacinda blink for two solid minutes when he'd first walked into her office that morning. "Not as bold as mine, of course, but still great. I mean you're *acting* weird. You should be thrilled about today. Everything's in place. The emerald is back. Pascowitz has decided you saved us all. The press and the public are fascinated. The auction is going to be a huge success."

"I'm just tired."

He winked broadly. "I guess so, with that studly Gideon Nash hanging about. How *is* Mr. Gorgeous?"

"Fine, I guess. In Paris."

"Ah." Andrew smiled. "Your personal hottie is out of town. Bummer. How about dinner later? I've hardly seen you in the past week."

"Sure."

Andrew paused, and she could feel his stare as she bent her head over a stack of paper she had no intention of reading. "Are you sure that's all that's wrong?"

Jacinda searched desperately for anger. Shouldn't she

be angry he skipped out on her? Shouldn't she be upset that she didn't mean enough to him to stay?

But all she felt was a kind of cold numbness.

Maybe he would be back, but he'd leave again. His abrupt departure that morning should be a wake-up call that if it wasn't over yet, it would be soon enough.

She wished she could think more practically instead of emotionally. Any sort of future between her and someone of Gideon's financial and social status was laughable, after all. Aligning her future with *any* man probably wasn't in the cards for her. She and Gideon had gotten together for hot sex; they'd parted still having hot sex.

What was so bad about that?

"It's not just great sex between you two, is it?" Andrew asked.

Her gaze jumped to his.

He smiled gently. "Remind me to tell you about George." Then he straightened and waved his hands dramatically. "I'm off for a mocha cappuccino, which I will bring to you, and you will drink. You will handle the press, the buyers, sellers and the rest of this day with your usual savvy professionalism." He headed for the door, turning back just before he exited. "Later, we'll eat fattening foods and remind each other how gorgeous, brilliant and witty we both are."

With a jaunty wave, he left, and tears flooded Jacinda's eyes. Her heart was shriveled in her chest, and she wanted nothing more than to lie her head on her desk and cry. She did have friends. Her job, which was her single most important life focus before Gideon had returned, was great. And today, she'd be the one behind the microphone at the one o'clock opening of her very first auction.

The fact that she'd rather be in a smoky French coffee-house trying to draw intel about a jewel-encrusted pipe from some informant was just something she'd have to get over.

She buried her pain deep inside and moved through her day. When she made the opening announcement for the auction—Mr. Pascowitz and the board members smiling from the front row—she felt a moment's exhilaration.

But the first items up for bid were the eagle-shaped bookends she and Gideon had unpacked a few days before.

The up and down of her emotions continued as the auction wore on. She was thrilled with the high-dollar sale of a painting by a somewhat obscure modern artist. She was disappointed at the low interest generated by an aging actress's twenties-era movie costume, which had amazing detail.

When the emerald was brought onstage, amid gasps and whispers, her whole body tightened, and she paced in the wings as the bidding commenced. It eventually sold for thirty percent more than its appraised value to a caller who chose not to be identified to the audience. And while Jacinda was certainly tempted to look at the name on the receipt, she didn't. After all she and that stone had been through together, just thinking about it being set into a piece of jewelry and worn by some unknown socialite made her want to throw up.

Gideon and Sophia had made the decision to let it go, even though, somehow, it still didn't seem right.

By the time the gavel fell for the last time, everyone at the auction house was clearly thrilled with the turnout and the receipts. Jacinda was exhausted.

Thankfully, after all the hand-shaking and back-patting, Andrew whisked her away to a favorite restaurant down the street, where two icy cold martinis were waiting on the bar.

"You're a good friend," she said as she toasted her assistant.

"And you're a crazy boss," he said, tapping their glasses gently. After sipping, he added, "Giving me the credit for holding the office together under the stress of the investigation was a bit much." He met her gaze over the rim of his glass. "If you remember, I spent most of the day after the emerald was stolen lying on the couch on your office, convinced the sky was falling."

Jacinda found her first genuine smile of the day. "But I laid a cold cloth on your head, and you got up. That's what you did for me today."

They dropped their heads sideways, each leaning on the other. "Friends."

"Forever," Jacinda finished.

"Someday, when we're lounging on the beach together, our toes in the sand, margaritas in our hands, you're going to explain the last week to me, right?"

"Absolutely."

As only good and true friends can manage, they shared their drink at the bar, then a great meal with very few questions and mostly a bunch of laughs. The restaurant staff had heard about the press hoopla over the emerald and its recovery that morning, so the manager offered them a free dessert, which they shared, dipping into raspberry and chocolate sauce with two spoons.

Jacinda's phone rang, as it had several times that day. She glanced at the display, expecting to see Gideon's number, but was surprised to see an unfamiliar local one. Wondering if someone from the auction house had a problem, she answered, "Jacinda Barrett."

"Hello, Jacinda, this is Sophia Graystone."

Jacinda nearly choked on her brownie. "Uh, hi... Sophia."

Andrew, who'd been trying to force the last bite of dessert into her mouth, clued in immediately to the change in her tone. He set the spoon aside, though his eyes were wild with curiosity.

"I need to talk to you right away," Sophia said.

"Ah, well...I'm a little...busy at the moment."

"What I have to say is important."

"But, I—"

"It concerns Gideon."

Feeling sick deep inside, Jacinda had no desire to talk about him, and the anger she'd hoped for finally emerged. It churned in her stomach and made her tone rude and abrupt. "He's gone."

"Gone?" Sophia echoed, sounding confused.

"He left."

There was a long pause. "He went to Paris on an assignment."

"Exactly." Her pulse hammered wildly. "He left."

"He'll be back," Sophia said.

Please. Fury and disappointment surged through Jacinda's body. "Will he? Will he really?"

Sophia sighed. "Where are you?"

"Why do you care?"

"Where are you?" Sophia asked again, calm when Jacinda was lost in her own anger and disappointment.

"Fitzgerald's, on Seventh."

"I'll be there in ten minutes."

Jacinda ended the call with a strange sense of unease and a stranger sense of comfort. Why would Gideon's grandmother give a crap about her if there wasn't something more important between her and Gideon than just a theft and an old secret? Maybe Sophia wanted to apologize in person, maybe she wanted to chat about art, or, maybe—more likely—Jacinda was just exhausted and reading too much in to everything today.

"Give it," Andrew said impatiently. "Who's coming?"

"Sophia Graystone."

"No freakin' kidding."

Jacinda gulped coffee. "No freakin' kidding."

"Is she coming to chase you away from her nephew, or convince you stay with him?"

Neither scenario seemed likely. She couldn't imagine Sophia lowering herself to do the first, and *Jacinda* staying didn't seem to be the problem between her and Gideon. "I have no idea."

Andrew started to rise, presumably attempting to scoot out of the booth. "Well, I think I'll let you two girls chat alone."

"Oh, no, you don't. I'm exhausted, depressed, angry and rapidly becoming despondent. You're not leaving."

"But if you two have a *personal* issue to discuss…"

"Since when has an issue being personal ever stopped you from butting in before?" She narrowed her eyes. "And since when are you scared of anybody?"

"I'm not scared," he said so quickly and with a rapid shake of his head, that she knew he was terrified.

"Me, either," she said, glancing around and wondering if she could pay the bill and escape before Sophia arrived.

"I vote we order some wine and bluff our way through."

"I second that," Jacinda said, raising her hand to get the waiter's attention.

GIDEON STOOD on his hotel balcony, watching the sun set on the quaint streetscape of rue Cler that somehow managed to be simple and genuine in the shadow cast by the Eiffel Tower.

After chasing down dead-end leads all day, he'd eaten at a local restaurant, then stopped by the wine shop for a bottle of Bordeaux and strolled by the fresh market for a small basket of seasonal berries. Without the flash of the Champs-Elysées or the tourists and artists of the area around the Louvre, rue Cler was typically Parisian. He'd stayed in this same hotel and watched this same scene dozens of times, and he'd enjoyed every moment of food, wine and conversation.

Tonight, he was miserable.

He should be with Jacinda, or Jacinda should be with him.

He'd known their relationship would come to this. He knew that he and Jacinda weren't just fun and games and that to continue being together one of them would have to compromise. And hadn't he decided the night they broke in to Gran's that she was worth a sacrifice?

But he, who charged into everything with confidence and no small amount of bravado, was uncertain.

What if things didn't work out? What if he moved to New York, and they were miserable together? What if their differences in outlook and goals were too much to overcome? What if she'd already changed her mind about being with him, or she was happy to let their relationship peter out? What if she could never find her own sense of self-worth and stop living in fear of the past?

He'd tried to call her several times that day, only to get her voice mail. He'd left messages that hadn't been returned. With the auction taking place, she had to have been busy, but he wanted to hear how things had gone. Was she pissed he'd left so suddenly? Was she glad he was gone?

And then there was the biggest question all—did he love her?

Paris seemed an appropriate place to discover the answer to that. But so far either his heart was the only part of him that was indecisive, or the Bordeaux had yet to reveal its secrets.

Either way, he was determined to uncover the answer.

JACINDA GRIPPED the stem of her wineglass and prayed she wouldn't burst into tears. "He's in Paris, Sophia. He's gone."

"He'll be back," she said for about the third time, then sipped her wine. "This is nice, by the way."

"Thank you," Jacinda said. "Andrew's choice."

Sophia beamed a dazzling smile on Andrew. "Of course it is. His father has impeccable taste as well."

Judging by the secret smile on Sophia's face, Jacinda wondered what else she knew about Andrew's father, who had been something of a playboy in his younger, bachelor days. Jacinda could picture Sophia flirting with that crowd.

"Father has always spoken of you with a special twinkle in his eyes," Andrew said, obviously mirroring her thoughts.

It was the oddest conversation. Sophia had come in quietly, with much less fanfare than when she had joined Jacinda and Gideon for dinner on Monday night. But then the crowd at Fitzgerald's was mostly working professionals, and they probably didn't realize they were in the presence of NYC royalty.

Jacinda and Andrew were playing polite hosts, making polite conversation, interspersed with comments about the most intimate relationship she'd ever had, while Andrew pretended to read the label on the wine bottle.

"Your father reminds me of Gideon," Sophia said. "So carefree and confident. But when he settled down, he did so for good. Isn't that right, Andrew?"

"Yes, ma'am."

"Andrew," Sophia said, giving him a bright smile and patting his hand, "would you mind finding our waiter and asking him if I could get a small snack? Just some cheese and crackers would do wonderfully."

"I, uh—" He glanced at Jacinda.

He was there to support her, but she could tell by the look on his face that he was about to leave her to her own devices—just like the first day Gideon had arrived at the auction house and Andrew neglected to make his "urgent" call to save her from herself.

"Sure," he said, practically flying from the booth.

As Jacinda watched him desert her, she decided she could blame this whole heartache-bound relationship with Gideon on Andrew. And wouldn't *that* keep her broken heart warm?

When he was gone, Sophia, naturally, wasted no time getting to the crux of things. "What happened to your unwavering belief in him?"

And she wasn't talking about Andrew.

Jacinda squirmed. "It wiggled."

The disappointed expression on Sophia's face said it all. Two nights ago Jacinda had stared down this woman in defense of Gideon. She'd accused her of several crimes, most of them felonies, simply on Gideon's word. She'd risked her career and reputation for him.

She hadn't worried about the consequences, or that a woman of Sophia's status should be laughing in the face of a former exotic dancer from Vegas. She'd treated Jacinda with the care and respect that Gideon always had.

What more proof did Jacinda need that she and Gideon shared a bond she'd never felt with anyone else in her entire life?

Her entire life.

Though they'd never talked about feelings or the future, he'd supported and cherished her. They'd worked together through some of the most difficult days of their lives. Was she really going to let that go?

The adventure of uncovering the emerald's origins had exhilarated her in a way she'd never expected. The stories Gideon had shared about his past cases had intrigued her, then fascinated her. His ever-changing lifestyle was something she'd never expected to want, but she had to admit that finding treasure, as opposed to parting with it, had taken on a new life. That actually seeing the world, as opposed to watching it pass by her office window, had become a serious need.

But if she admitted she wanted to accept her own call to adventure, if she admitted she wanted him, she had to hold out her heart to him without knowing it would be accepted. She had to convince herself that she *deserved* to be accepted.

"He loves you," Sophia said suddenly, quietly.

"No. I—"Jacinda swallowed. "Do you really think so?"

"Yes. And you love him." Sophia's gaze blazed into Jacinda's. "One of you has to take the next step."

"I'm scared."

"I bet. You have reason to be. Love isn't easy." Sophia smiled. "But it's worth it. I was counting on my grandson to be the one to take a chance. Heaven knows, he's never hesitated before."

Butterflies in Jacinda's stomach took flight. "But he is now." Hell, he hadn't just hesitated. He'd run.

"You're thinking he's not in Paris just to look for some old pipe."

"He's not."

"No. He's working through his feelings, as you are." Sophia raised her glass in a toast. "See how well you know him? Nobody ever understood him that way before. Not his parents, his friends and certainly not any other woman he's been involved with."

"*You* understand him."

She sipped her wine. "You think that makes us competitors?"

"No, I just—" Jacinda's gaze dropped to the cluster of rubies circling Sophia's index finger, and her stomach plummeted. What was she doing here with this woman? "I want you to like me."

She leaned forward, squeezing Jacinda's hand. "I do."

It couldn't be that simple, could it?

Somehow, staring into the kindness of Sophia's face, Jacinda realized she didn't need to fear the exposure of her past. She simply needed to accept it as part of her, a part that she'd always have and never fully escape.

But that was okay.

"I used to be an exotic dancer in Vegas," she blurted out.

"I know, dear."

Jacinda swallowed. "You knew Sunday night when I came to dinner."

"Of course. I admire you for getting what you want without money and power. It's something I've always had and have used as a crutch at times. You *have* to be proud of what you've accomplished."

"I am." And maybe for the first time she truly was. Maybe, in thinking she'd be judged for her past, she'd been the one doing the judging. But she also wanted to get across an important point to Sophia. "I don't care about Gideon's money. Your money. Or whoever's."

"I'm sure you don't. I imagine it would be easier, simpler if he was, well, not penniless, but at least a man of more normal means. Then you'd be on an equal field."

"How would you know—"

"I know because that's how I'd feel. We're not so different, Jacinda. I'd like to think that's why Gideon values you so much."

As Jacinda fought the urge to drop her jaw while being compared to Sophia Graystone by the woman herself, Sophia leaned back in the booth with her wineglass. "But you do care about the power, as does Gideon. You're both used to having things your way. If you're going to be together and make your relationship work, you've got to stop thinking that way. One of you has to take that protection off your heart first."

"You think it should be me?"

"I do. Otherwise, I'd be on a plane to Paris right now preparing to have this conversation with him." She angled her head. "Maybe *you* should think about a hop over the pond."

She couldn't just *hop* on a plane. That *pond* involved nearly a half a day's flight and a huge time change. She had responsibilities at work. She had to wrap up the press from the auction. She had to make sure—

What *was* more important than her happiness? Than finding a purpose in life that didn't involve covering up or making up for her past? For making sure everybody else's day and life went smoothly no matter now much it cost her?

For once she had the urge to chuck her responsibilities.

She pictured Gideon—his eyes glowing so brightly it made the spectacular emerald they'd all chased look dull—as he'd knelt in front of his grandmother's safe, in search of treasure and the truth. She remembered the intense, but still gentle look on his face when he stared at her just before their bodies became one. She smiled over the unspoken communication they always seemed to have.

"I love him so much it scares me," she admitted to Sophia.

"I know, though it's nice to hear you say it. I also know things between you two have been fast and intense, and I know there are a lot of things to work out, but I'd be honored to have you as part of our family someday."

Jacinda blinked back a rush of tears. "Thanks. You guys are pretty great yourselves." She paused. "As long as you don't try to steal any more big rocks."

Sophia's eyes twinkled. "I promise."

"You don't have any more deep, dark family secrets, do you?"

"Mmm. Well…"

Jacinda had the feeling that whatever her future held, she'd find it entwined with the Sophia Graystones of the world. They were, oddly enough, her kind of people. "If Gideon and I were to ever get married, can we have McElvy as a wedding present?"

Sophia laughed. "Not a chance, darling. Not a chance."

14

JACINDA LEFT her dinner with Sophia, mildly chastised Andrew for abandoning her—though if she managed to convince Gideon how amazing they were together, she'd likely have to name her first child after him—went home and booked a flight for Paris.

Since the flight didn't leave until 6:00 p.m. the following day, she rushed in to work on Thursday morning and told Mr. Pascowitz she'd like a leave of absence to pursue her sudden urge to travel. Surprisingly, instead of firing her, he'd smiled benignly and said the auction house staff could always use more overseas exposure and maybe they could work out a brokering fee if she found clients interested in selling their treasures at the auction house.

Though Jacinda suspected Sophia had either charmed or bullied her boss into submission, she didn't waste time wondering or debating.

She spent the day shopping.

It wasn't every day that a woman chased a man as extraordinary as Gideon Nash—well, at least a woman who was her—and she intended to make it count.

She'd bought lingerie, of course, as well as a kick-ass red leather jacket she thought would look amazing on a treasure hunt through any country, plus she'd found the perfect sexy-but-classy dress to wear when she showed up unannounced at his hotel in Paris. When she walked into his room wearing the emerald green satin, halter top, cut-down-to-*there* ensemble, complete with spectacular gold shoes that Sophia's personal shopper had recommended, she had no doubt that Gideon Michael Nash would drop his jaw and declare his undying love.

Well, hopefully.

As she held the handles of her shopping bags, riding the elevator toward her apartment, an excitement she hadn't allowed herself to feel in a long time consumed her. The future was bright and hopeful, and, damn it, nothing was going to bring her down. Even herself.

She opened the door to her apartment, dropped her bags in the foyer, then raced toward her bedroom. Surely she had time to shower before—

"What?" Gideon asked, "no welcome-back kiss?"

Jacinda literally braced her hand against the wall to stop her momentum. She glanced back at the man standing in the middle of her living room. She blinked. "You're supposed to be in Paris."

Gideon, gorgeous in faded jeans and a black T-shirt, his bright green eyes focused on hers, held out his arms. "I'm not."

"But—" Her whole body went soft and needy even as her brain questioned his presence. It had been so long since he'd touched her. She really needed his touch. She needed the heat only the two of them could generate.

Still, she had *plans*. "Have you talked to your grandmother today?"

"No. Is she—"

"She's fine. But why are you back—"

"So soon? Well…" His gaze fixed on hers, he walked toward her, grabbing her hand and tugging her into his arms. "I decided I couldn't live without you another day."

Jacinda's heart jumped. Good grief. Sophia and Andrew had been right. All her dreams were about to come true. "Damn it."

"What?"

"There's a dress. Damn it, there's a dress for this moment."

As much as she wanted to hear what he had to say, she pushed her way out of his arms. Everything needed to be perfect. She had it all planned out.

She reached into her purse and tossed her plane reservations on the coffee table. She hoped that would be enough to hold him until she was ready, then ran from the room, clutching hope and her shopping bags in both hands.

She was coming to him.

Gideon stared at Jacinda's travel itinerary for several minutes before realizing it was actually real.

After all the risk to her job and reputation, after his indecision, their combined claims of fun and no commitment. After the craziness of the auction, the police interrogations, the B&E, she'd planned to come to him. She wanted more than what had happened in Vegas. She wanted him.

Maybe he was just a man, but the dress seemed superfluous.

He walked down the hall toward her bedroom and gave two quick taps on the door. "I don't care if you're ready."

"I do!" she shouted back.

"I don't care what you're wearing. I want to talk to you."

"You will. In just a minute."

He had the urge to pound his head against the door. He'd flown three thousand miles to get back to her, and she wanted to try on clothes.

As the cats wound their way around his ankles, he reached down and scratched their heads. "I know, fellas. She hasn't even noticed you yet."

And they'd dressed up for the occasion, in a couple million in emeralds. Lochy wore the bracelet around his neck, and the ring dangled from a chain around Ralph's neck. The Graystone family emerald was back where it belonged—at least parts of it.

When the door finally opened, Gideon straightened, ready to complain about not even getting to kiss her before she'd disappeared. His mouth opened as usual, but then he couldn't seem to close it.

Jacinda wore a satin, emerald-green, body-hugging dress that dipped way low between her breasts. Gold, high-heeled sparkly shoes put a good four inches on her height and made her legs look about a mile long. Her lips were glossy, her eyes smoky.

"You're gonna match the jewelry," he managed to say around his swollen tongue.

"Thank— What jewelry?"

He pointed down at the cats.

Jacinda glanced down, then her gaze shot back to his. "Are they wearing emeralds?"

He nodded.

"*The* emerald? But it was sold to—"

"An anonymous buyer on the phone. That was me. I had a jeweler break up the stone into smaller pieces."

His body finally managed to override his stunned brain, and he stepped forward to pull her into his arms. "You're the most beautiful woman I've ever seen," he said huskily, then kissed her, long and deep.

"Are those emeralds for me or the cats?" she asked when he leaned back.

He stroked her cheek. "Greedy all of a sudden, are we?"

"Well, they're not my cats."

"Good point." He clutched her hand, and they knelt beside the cats together. "I figured if you were super pissed at me, you'd still accept the jewelry rather than let the cats run around with it forever."

"I *was* angry," she said as he unfastened the bracelet from around Lochy's neck, then wrapped it around her wrist. "At first. I thought you weren't coming back."

His gaze jumped to hers. "Of course I was…" He let his protest fall away. When had he ever promised her a future? When had he taken the time to explain everything he was feeling and wonder if she felt the same? "I'm sorry," he said simply.

"It's okay. It's just that I have these trust issues…"

"I know, and I had lousy timing. I'm used to taking off whenever I need to. I'm not used to having someone waiting for me." He slid the chain off Ralph's neck, and the cat batted at it while Gideon tried to unhook the chain. "That's all going to have to change, though." With the ring finally loose, he slid it on Jacinda's finger, the middle one of her right hand. He'd like to move it one finger over and on the other hand, but he figured it was best to take things slowly for a while.

"Let's call it a commitment ring," he said, drawing her

to her feet and trying to talk around the lump of emotion crowding his throat. "No matter where I am or what I'm doing, I'm always thinking of you. And you can always count on me to come back to you. Always." He cupped her cheek. "I love you, Jacinda."

She laid her hand over his. "And I love you, Gideon."

He grinned. "That makes this moment so much better. I was half afraid when you found me here you'd try to toss me out on my butt."

"Nah. Though it was a good thing you didn't show up yesterday."

"I knew I'd better show up with a gift." He held her hands by her fingertips, looking down at the sparkling gems that had brought them together. "They suit you. I knew they would." In fact, when he'd picked them up on the way here, the moment he saw them, he knew he loved her. He knew she, and only she, would make something that had caused so much pain beautiful again.

"I can't believe you broke up the stone," she said. "I can't believe you *bought* the stone."

"Yeah, well, you might want to suck up to Pascowitz a bit longer and keep your job, since I'm a few million in the hole. That's only fifteen karats of the stone, and I'd been planning to sell the other six and donate the proceeds, but…" He trailed off as he noticed her face had turned pale. "What's wrong?"

"I, ah, sort of took a leave of absence from my job. I'm not sure exactly when or where my next paycheck is coming from."

"You're leaving Callibro's?"

"I was coming to join you." Her eyes lit up. "Did you find the pipe? I was really hoping you hadn't yet, because

I was doing some research, and I found an old club where the members used to smoke these elaborate—"

He started laughing.

Clearly confused, she stared at him. "You didn't find the pipe?"

"Not yet," he said, still caught up in laughter.

"But there's a funny story about the pipe?"

He shook his head.

"Mmm, well, since we're in a financial crunch, I'm thinking we should get a little more *serious* about finding the pipe."

"I was kidding about the money." He waved his hand, realizing that Jacinda had genuinely thought he didn't have any more money and hadn't blinked an eye. He'd gotten his wish to be genuinely loved for himself. "I've got plenty of money. I'm laughing because I rented an office this morning. I'm hiring a secretary. I was thinking of writing a book or becoming a consultant for a university. I'm staying here."

"*O-kay.* Why?"

"Because you're here." He kissed her, savoring the feel of her body against his as he never had before. "I was miserable on my adventure, looking for that damn pipe. If you're not with me, I can't do it anymore."

"So I was ready to give up my security to come to you, and you were willing to give up your adventures to stay with me?"

"Looks like it."

"So now what are we going to do? I really wanted to go to Paris, Gideon. I shopped. I'm packed."

"We'll do both, of course. Maybe six months each. That's fair, right?"

"As long as we go to Paris first."

He buried his face in her hair, holding her tight against his chest. "That sounds perfect."

* * * * *

Enjoy a sneak preview of
MATCHMAKING WITH A MISSION
by B.J. Daniels,
part of the WHITEHORSE, MONTANA *miniseries.*
Available from Harlequin Intrigue
in April 2008.

Nate Dempsey has returned to Whitehorse to uncover the truth about his past...

Nate sensed someone watching the house and looked out in surprise to see a woman astride a paint horse just on the other side of the fence. He quickly stepped back from the filthy second-floor window, although he doubted she could have seen him. Only a little of the June sun pierced the dirty glass to glow on the dust-coated floor at his feet as he waited a few heartbeats before he looked out again.

The place was so isolated he hadn't expected to see another soul. Like the front yard, the dirt road was waist-high with weeds. When he'd broken the lock on the back door, he'd had to kick aside a pile of rotten leaves that had blown in from last fall.

As he sneaked a look, he saw that she was still there, staring at the house in a way that unnerved him. He shielded his eyes from the glare of the sun off the dirty window and studied her, taking in her head of long blond hair that feathered out in the breeze from under her Western straw hat.

She wore a tan canvas jacket, jeans and boots. But it

was the way she sat astride the brown-and-white horse that nudged the memory.

He felt a chill as he realized he'd seen her before. In that very spot. She'd been just a kid then. A kid on a pretty paint horse. Not this one—the markings were different. Anyway, it couldn't have been the same horse, considering the last time he had seen her was more than twenty years ago. That horse would be dead by now.

His mind argued it probably wasn't even the same girl. But he knew better. It was the way she sat on the horse, so at home in a saddle and secure in her world on the other side of that fence.

To the boy he'd been, she and her horse had represented freedom, a freedom he'd known he would never have—even after he escaped this house.

Nate saw her shift in the saddle, and for a moment he feared she planned to dismount and come toward the house. With Ellis Harper in his grave, there would be little to keep her away.

To his relief, she reined her horse around and rode back the way she'd come.

As he watched her ride away, he thought about the way she'd stared at the house—today and years ago. While the smartest thing she could do was to stay clear of this house, he had a feeling she'd be back.

Finding out her name should prove easy, since he figured she must live close by. As for her interest in Harper House… He would just have to make sure it didn't become a problem.

* * * * *

Be sure to look for
MATCHMAKING WITH A MISSION
and other suspenseful Harlequin Intrigue stories,
available in April
wherever books are sold.

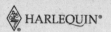

nocturne™

The Bloodrunners
trilogy continues with book #2.

The hunt meant more to Jeremy Burns than dominance—
it meant facing the woman he left behind. Once
Jillian Murphy had belonged to Jeremy, but now she was
the Spirit Walker to the Silvercrest wolves. It would take
more than the rights of nature for Jeremy to renew his
claim on her—and she would not go easily once he had.

LAST WOLF
HUNTING

by RHYANNON BYRD

Available in April wherever books are sold.

Be sure to watch out for the last book,
Last Wolf Watching, available in May.

SN61785

REQUEST YOUR FREE BOOKS!

2 FREE NOVELS PLUS 2 FREE GIFTS!

HARLEQUIN®

Blaze™

Red-hot reads!

HB08

HARLEQUIN® *Blaze*™

introduces...

Lust in Translation
A sexy new international miniseries.

Don't miss the first book...

FRENCH KISSING
by **Nancy Warren**

April 2008

N.Y. fashionista Kimi Renton knows sexy
photographer Holden McGregor is a
walking fashion disaster. And she's tried
to make him over. But when they're
lip-locked, it's ooh-la-la all the way!

LUST IN TRANSLATION
Because sex is the same
in any language!

HARLEQUIN®
Blaze™

COMING NEXT MONTH

www.eHarlequin.com

HBCNM0308